Wild Horses
and
Wild Cattle

RANDELL WHALEY

PAGE PUBLISHING, INC.
Conneaut Lake, PA

First originally published by Page Publishing 2020

ISBN 978-1-6624-0861-8 (pbk)
ISBN 978-1-6624-0862-5 (digital)

Printed in the United States of America

CHAPTER 1

Going Mustanging

Jim watched his fire get going good as he added more twigs and pieces of tree branches to it. It was November, and there was snow everywhere. He had just finished unsaddling and hobbling his horses and had started making camp. He'd have to sleep in the snow tonight. But he'd slept in the snow before. Quite a few times, in fact.

He kept on adding more fuel to the fire, gradually moving up to bigger pieces until he had it going strong enough to start adding pieces of log about four inches thick or so. At first, the snow sizzled around it.

He had gathered driftwood from the nearby trees. Then he found a dead tree that was small enough that he could drag it up near the fire. He took his ax and cut the trunk of it into good-sized logs about three feet long. They ranged from about three to five inches thick.

Then he sliced some beef off a carcass he had hanging from a nearby tree and came back and rigged a tripod over the fire so he could get a chunk of meat suspended in the middle to start broiling. He had killed a maverick calf earlier in the day, so he had fresh camp meat.

Jim was medium height and medium weight. He had brown hair and blue eyes. He was wearing batwing chaps and a sheepskin coat. He had taken off his gloves when he started cooking.

He had just returned from a trail drive to Kansas with a herd of Rolling J cattle. When the Rolling J crew returned to Texas, he drew his pay, saddled up one of his two personal horses, and rode into Waco leading his spare horse. He stopped at the General Store and bought the supplies he thought he'd need. Then he set out for southwest Texas. He had decided to spend the winter months wild-horse hunting.

It was still daylight by a couple of hours. He saw a rider coming toward his camp. He was wearing batwing chaps and a sheepskin coat just like Jim's. Jim wore his six-gun on the left side for a cross draw. He had formed the habit of doing so because, otherwise, it got in the way of his roping. He saw just that lone rider with a packhorse following and no one else. There were a couple of hundred yards of open space to the north from where the rider was approaching. And he appeared to be alone. So he just kept his hand near his gun and waited until he rode up.

The rider kept on riding until he was about twenty yards away and stopped. "Hello, the fire," he called. "I'm riding friendly."

Jim thought he recognized that voice from a couple of years ago. While his cavalry outfit was evacuating Richmond, as a matter of fact! So he stood up to greet him. He recognized his face now.

"Jack Watkins, you old outlaw!" he exclaimed. Jack rode on up and dismounted. He recognized Jim by now too. He took off the glove on his right hand and reached out to grab Jim's hand and shook it vigorously. "It's good to see you."

"It's good to see you too," Jack replied. "I see you survived the war after all."

"There were times when I had reason to have my doubts about it, but I did make it. You riding for an outfit these days?"

"Nope. They let everyone go they didn't need. So I'm riding the grub line."

"Well, I've got beef," which was obvious. Jack could see the beef broiling over the fire; plus he could see the carcass of the steer calf hanging from a nearby tree. "I shot a maverick just a couple of hours ago. So the meat'll be good and fresh."

"I've got flour for biscuits," Jack replied.

So Jack unsaddled his horses and took them out to where Jim's two horses were pawing the snow and grazing. He hobbled them and turned them loose with Jim's horses. They had to paw the snow away enough so they could reach grass to graze. Jack had the same build as Jim but was a couple of inches shorter.

So Jim had help cooking supper this night. He went to the carcass and cut off another sizable chunk of meat and rigged it over the fire so he'd have enough meat for two people. Then he got a pot of beans started. He pulled out a side of bacon and sliced off one slice, cut it in two, and put it in the beans for flavoring. He already had a pot of coffee brewed. So Jim sat on a log and Jack sat on a nearby rock and they started drinking coffee and yarning. Each one of them rolled a cigarette and lit it, puffing the smoke with relish. When the beans and meat were nearly done, Jack made up a pan of biscuits and put them in a Dutch oven he had with his gear. He took a twig and maneuvered some of the coals off to one side of the fire. He sat the Dutch oven over the coals and then took two twigs and picked some coals up to put on the lid of the Dutch oven. In about ten or fifteen minutes, they'd have some hot biscuits. When Jim saw Jack getting the biscuits on, he put a small amount of grease in a skillet, poured in some flour, added water, and started stirring it. They'd have gravy too.

As good a vittles as you'd find at any cow camp, Jim decided. They both ate with an appetite. There's something about riding all day that makes a man hungry.

"You say you're riding the grub line," Jim mentioned. "You really looking for work on just seeing new country?"

"Actually, I'm not looking for work right now," Jack answered. "I have my own spread a little southwest of here. But I don't have enough cattle to make a go of it yet. So I worked as a cowhand during the summer so I could eat regular and draw some wages. After the war, I found out the money I did have saved was worthless 'cause it was Confederate money. So I'm having to start all over again. But I don't have enough horses with my outfit either. I figured I'd head out to West Texas and go mustang hunting this winter."

"That's where I'm headed," Jim responded. "And I need a partner."

"We'd really need about five or six men to run mustangs," Jack replied. "Four would be a minimum."

"We could hire them" was Jim's answer to that.

"If we had the wages to pay them" was Jack response.

"Yes, we'd have to have that." Jim had his summer's wages. He didn't blow in his money like most other cowboys did. But he had already bought himself a grubstake. So some of his money had already been used for that. He didn't have enough money to pay wages to any cowboys. "But we could probably find a couple more cowboys to throw in with us as partners."

"Yep, I'm sure we could," Jack said. "Especially this time of year. There'll be quite a few cowboys looking for work."

They kept drinking coffee and swapping lies until it got to be time to roll into their blankets. They each had a ground cloth and tarp to keep their bedding dry in the snow. It would keep the snow from melting against their blankets due to their body heat.

They saw no need to post a watch. They were only about fifteen miles or so south of Waco in an area populated with farms because it was near the Brazos River. So they didn't anticipate any trouble. If anyone did approach, their horses would smell the other horses and whinny. So they got inside their blankets and went to sleep. They slept sound as a log all night.

Vickie Marie Allen

The hardest thing Jim had to do so far this year was to say goodbye to
Vickie Allen again. She was not only the most beautiful woman Jim
had ever seen but the only woman he cared about seeing.

Vickie had blond hair and blue eyes and dimples that showed
when she smiled. She was 5 feet, 5 inches in height and weighed 125
pounds. Jim had fallen in love with her instantly at a barbeque dinner
that the town of Culpepper had put on for General J. E. B. Stuart's
cavalry brigade in June 1863. They had a dance out on the grass on
the outskirts of town that night, and he found young Vickie there
with her parents. She was only thirteen years old at the time. Jim
had barely turned sixteen. He had lied about his age to get into the
army. He danced every dance with her that night. When he got back
to where his regiment was camped, he couldn't sleep for several hours
because he was so happy.

Jim had just joined the Confederate Army a week previously.
After returning late from the dance that night, he heard bugles sound
before daylight the following morning. He found himself embroiled
in battle within minutes. It was a battle on horseback with sabers
against the mounted cavalry of the enemy. He survived his first battle, but after that, he went to see Vickie every time he could finagle
a pass or furlough. So their romance blossomed and waxed strong.
After the war's end, Jim found the plantation he had grown up on
reduced to ashes. He decided to go west and build himself a future
out there. He promised Vickie he'd send for her.

But Vickie was a resourceful young lady in her own right. She was fifteen by then and considered herself old enough to get married. And she didn't want anyone but Jim. So she prevailed on her father, who owned a grocery / dry goods store, to sell his store and move west so she could be near Jim.

Vickie had blossomed into a ravishing beauty by this time. The cowboys in Texas couldn't resist her. But she was true to her man, and the cowboys all finally figured out she simply wasn't available and accepted it.

Toward the end of the summer of 1866, the Rolling J Ranch where Jim worked had taken a herd of cattle up to Abilene to the railroad to sell. When Jim returned about two months or so later, he had his summer's wages in his pocket. And he had two horses. But that was it. He couldn't see how he could get married until he figured out a way to support a wife.

He had heard that the western part of Texas was covered with wild mustangs and had almost no people—almost no white men, at least. And he knew there was a good market for mustangs now that cattle drives to Kansas had become practical.

He rode up to the Allen's General Store and tied his horses to the hitch rail. He walked inside. He saw Vickie at the cash register waiting on a customer. She looked up and saw him. He hadn't shaved in weeks and looked a little rangy, but she was thrilled to see him.

"Jim!" she squealed and ran around the counter and jumped into his arms. The customer looked around to see what was going on. Then he grinned. He was a grizzled old cow camp cook and was buying supplies for the ranch he was working for. He had a gray beard and gray hair.

Jim had about a three weeks' beard but had combed his hair that morning. He removed his hat, of course, just before walking into the store. He had dropped it on the floor when Vickie grabbed him. And he still had on his chaps.

Mr. Allen heard the commotion from his office, so he came out and finished checking out the customer. Then he walked over to where Jim and Vickie were standing and held out his hand to shake hands with him. Jim managed to get one hand free to take Mr. Allen's hand.

"So you're back from your drive," Mr. Allen said.

"Yes, just got back today."

"Will you have dinner with us tonight?" Mr. Allen then asked.

"Yes, he will," Vickie answered for him. "And, Papa, can I have the rest of the day off?"

Mr. Allen knew that would be her next question, so he just said sure. But he knew there'd be more business than usual today if a crew of cowhands had just returned from a drive.

Jim sort of figured this out, so he said, "I need to go take care of my horses. Then I need to get a shave and haircut and bath. You can stay here and help your father mind the store until then." But he promised he'd be at the Allens' house for dinner. He picked up his hat off the floor before he walked out. His spurs jingled a little as he walked out the door.

Jim showed up shortly after six o'clock. He put his horses in the stalls behind the house and unsaddled them before he walked back around to the front of the house and knocked on the door. And he had left his chaps and spurs with his saddle. He normally didn't wear them indoors.

Shortly, he was seated at the table with Vicki and her mama and papa. Everyone was obviously very glad that he was back. He now looked especially handsome with his new haircut and shave. He had managed to change into clean clothes when he got his bath at the bathhouse.

They started eating. It was rib eye steak with all the trimmings. You'd expect no less at the Allen house.

"How was your drive?" was the first question Vicki asked.

"It went fine. Hot and dusty." He wasn't going to tell her about the fight with Indians or the two cowboys that were killed in stampedes. "How did things go here?"

"Fine" was her answer.

"There's lots of herds of wild horses in the western part of the state," Jim said simply. "And I can homestead 2,048 acres of land. I want to start a horse ranch as I mentioned to you before. I could go catch some wild horses and get a horse herd that way."

Vicki didn't like what was apparently coming. She had moved all the way from Virginia to Texas to be with her man.

"I can take the money I made on the drive and use it to buy a remuda of horses and a grubstake. That would get me started."

Vickie started looking somewhat downcast. She knew this meant he'd be leaving again. And Vickie was tired of him leaving. Seemed like all he had done since she'd met him was leave! She wished he would come back and *not* leave just once!

After dinner, Vickie brought Jim his mandolin. She kept it for him when he was on the drive. He was afraid it would get busted. She sat down at the piano, and they played and sang the old songs they loved so well. They had a guest room, so he stayed the night.

The following morning, he saddled up his horses, put on his chaps and spurs, and rode to the General Store. He bought his grub-stake and went to the cash register to pay. Vickie accepted his money. Then he went out and loaded it onto his packhorse. When he was ready to go, Vickie clung to him as if for dear life and wouldn't let him go. He just held her and put his cheek against her golden hair and told her how much he loved her. He figured he could at least do that.

But then, after several minutes, he mounted up and rode out of town. That was after promising her he'd be back in the spring and explaining to her that he wouldn't be able to write very often since there'd be no towns or post offices where he'd be going.

Vickie walked to the southeast corner of the store and watched Jim ride south. She kept watching until he was out of sight. Just before he disappeared over a rise, he stopped and wheeled his horse and looked back. He saw she was still standing there. He knew she would be. He waved and she waved back. Then he disappeared over the rise.

Vickie bowed her head as she walked back to the store. It was hard seeing her man leave again. And she was tired of seeing him leave. But he always came back. She'd have to grant him that. He always came back, and he'd come back this time. She fondled the golden necklace that hung around her neck. It had a locket with Jim's picture in it. She had insisted on getting their pictures made one time in Virginia when Jim had come to see her when on leave. They had a couple of poses of them setting together. But she also had individual shots made of herself and Jim. And she prevailed on the photographer to make her one print small enough to fit in her locket. Jim had the individual picture of her, and he carried it in his pocket. The necklace that held the locket was a gift that Jim bought for her while still in Virginia.

Jim rode south until the middle of the afternoon when he saw a weaning-sized maverick calf. It apparently had missed the branding of any of the ranches around, so it was fair pickings for any rancher or cowboy that could slap its brand on him. Or shoot him and use him for camp meat, which was what Jim had done.

So when it came morning, Jack and Jim broke camp, saddled up, and headed southwest across the snow-covered prairies.

Joe Williams and Sam Blake

Joe Williams had decided to leave his South Carolina plantation. The bank refused his request for a loan to hire cotton choppers. And it was too much land to hoe it all himself. He had been unable to make his payments during the war since the field's hands had abandoned it and it went to weeds. On his return from the war the previous summer, he had plowed it and planted it himself. But when he sold his cotton the previous fall, it didn't bring enough to make his mortgage payment. So he was about three years behind in his payments. A carpetbagger from a northern state had bought out the bank the previous year when it nearly went broke. So he had a new banker who wasn't the slightest bit sympathetic to the cause of the Southern planter.

As a result, Joe wasn't surprised two weeks later when he found out that the bank was foreclosing on his plantation and had scheduled an auction to sell it.

Joe had brown hair and gray eyes and was of a slender build. He weighed about 140 pounds or so. He had returned home to his South Carolina plantation a year and a half previously to find his plantation in weeds. He found his plow horses still in their pasture unmolested, much to his surprise, and he immediately started plowing and getting ready to plant his cotton crop. He got his crop planted too late that first year and didn't make as good a crop as he otherwise would have. He hired field hands to pick the cotton. It would be impossible to pick it before winter by himself. After he paid his field hands, he didn't have enough money left to meet the mortgage payment.

Now this year wasn't any different.

Joe and his father had worked this farm before the war. His mother had died giving birth to him, so his only family had been his father. Then he learned that his father had been killed at Shiloh. He was back from the war himself now, and it was just him.

Joe remembered Sam Blake, who was at Appomattox with him when General Lee surrendered his Army to General Grant. He also remembered his other friend, Lieutenant Jim Bennett. Jim had decided to go west and start a ranch. He wondered how he was doing.

He had refused to allow them to place his personal horse on the mortgage. But in the foreclosure process, he lost his plow horses. So he saddled up his gray and rode over to Sam Blake's place.

Sam Blake was always a little paunchy about the waist until the last part of the war in which everyone became rather lank with the short rations they had to get by with. Sam had dark-brown hair and brown eyes. He was about the same height as Joe. That he was always pleasant company was what Joe mainly remembered. And he liked to drink and gamble.

He rode up to the yard of Sam's place. He called out to see if he was home. Sam opened the door and walked outside. Sam had a smaller place than Joe's. He only had about eighty acres compared to the two-hundred-acre plantation that Joe had owned.

Joe dismounted to shake hands with Sam.

"Howdy, Sam. It's good to see you!" he said.

"It's good to see you too," Sam said with a big grin on his face. Joe walked to the corral to unsaddle his horse and put him inside. It was nearly noon. Sam had already started cooking dinner.

After Joe made sure his horse had water and some hay, he came back to Sam's cabin.

"Come in and set," Sam told him. "Chow will be ready before long."

Sam had some pork chops on the stove frying and some potatoes boiling. He opened the door to the stove and put another chunk of wood in it.

Then he sat down at the table, packed his pipe, and lit it. Joe didn't pack his pipe, so he handed him his tobacco. He could put two and two together. Joe obviously appreciated the smoke.

"How did your crop do last year?" Sam asked him.

"After I paid my cotton pickers, I didn't have much left," Joe answered.

"Not too much different for me, but I did make a little money," Sam told him. "It's been dry this summer, so it doesn't look like I'll make much of a crop this year." Sam got up to turn the pork chops.

Sam's land wasn't mortgaged. So he wasn't in any danger of losing it. He had inherited it from his parents. They were both dead now. They died of smallpox when he was fifteen years old.

"I'm planning to sell my place this fall. I have a buyer. One of my neighbors wants to add it to his place. Prices are down now, but I think it will be better than nothing."

Sam got up to turn the pork chops again and decided they were done. He got two plates out of the cupboard and put the two pork chops on them, then took up the potatoes. Then he poured coffee for both of them. They had themselves a good, old-fashioned Southern meal.

"So they took your place away from you?" Sam asked. Joe had mentioned to him he was about to lose his place the last time he saw him.

"Yes, I'm without a home now."

"Well you can stay here with me. You can help me do some repair work on the barn. I'll get a better price for it if everything looks like it's in a good shape."

So Joe stayed on, and he and Sam repaired the roof on the barn and walked around the perimeter of the property looking for places where the fence needed work. Then they went out and started hoeing the cotton. It hadn't grown much due to a lack of rain, but it hadn't shriveled up and died either.

"I figure I won't go looking for my buyer. It would not be good if he thought I was too eager to sell," Sam told Joe. "I'll just wait until he comes by again."

It was another week before the buyer did come by again. Joe and Sam were out in the field hoeing when they saw him ride up in his buggy pulled by a shiny black gelding.

Joe and Sam walked up to the house when they saw him coming down the road. He was there waiting for them when they got to the house.

"Are you ready to sell?" His name was Matt Gardner. Sam had known him for years.

"That depends on how much you're willing to pay." Sam knew he'd better be cagey.

"Land isn't worth much right now. And I can see you aren't likely to make a crop this year. Doesn't look like you're going to make enough to make your mortgage payment."

"I don't have a mortgage payment," retorted Sam.

That was something that Matt didn't know. "Then why do want to sell?"

"I don't necessarily want to sell. But I'm thinking I might go West and try my luck out there. So it would be better to just sell this place if I'm going to look for a new start someplace else."

The bickering continued for another hour before Matt finally made an offer. Sam pretended not to be interested. "Joe and I really need to go back to hoeing. But I thank you for coming out."

"I'll give you seven dollars an acre. And that's more than it's worth."

"That's not more than its worth, but I might not get much more than that. I'll take it," Sam told him.

So a few days later, Sam and Joe rode into town to the bank and closed the deal. He took the money in cash. Then he and Joe rode back to the farm to pack up and get ready to leave.

*****

So in the middle of July 1866, just when the weather was the hottest, Joe and Sam saddled up, loaded down Sam's two packhorses with grub and supplies, and started their long ride to Texas. It was a hot day when they headed their horses down the road to the west. Sam had stocked up on supplies the day before, so they had enough grub to last them a few weeks.

Cards and Drink

Joe and Sam arrived at Waco in November. There was snow on the ground. They saw a hotel and stopped. They tied their horses at the hitch rail and went in. They decided to go to the restaurant and order. The waitress came to wait on them. She was a beautiful brunette with a full dress reaching to the floor. It had a high neckline and long sleeves, but she still looked enticing. Her dark-brown hair was piled up on her head. "And what's your name?" Joe asked.

"Jeannie," she answered.

"You're the best-looking thing I've seen in months," he told her.

Jeannie blushed. Joe was a mighty fine-looking man. And Sam, too, for that matter.

"What do you want to order?" she asked.

Both of them ordered. In a few minutes, Jeannie brought their food—fried steak and potatoes, beans, biscuits and gravy, and hot coffee. And they appreciated the coffee. It was nice to be able to have coffee anytime you wanted it.

After they had eaten, they decided to go to a saloon next door. They went to the bar and ordered a whiskey each. They hadn't had anything to drink in weeks. They had mostly just camped wherever they stopped for the night on their long ride West. Sam saw a card game going on at a table nearby. He walked over and started watching the game. Joe saw a saloon girl standing nearby and walked over and started talking to her. She had on a floor-length dress with one side tied up to show off a beautiful knee. And her shoulders were bare, and her dress had a dip-and-dare neckline showing a little cleavage. She looked delicious. Joe offered to buy her a drink. She accepted with a beautiful smile.

In a few minutes, Joe saw that Sam had joined the card game. He wasn't surprised. Joe hoped he didn't lose all his money. Sam had some money left from selling his farm in South Carolina. He turned his attention back to the beautiful young thing standing beside him. He had learned her name was Betsy.

"So how long have you lived in Waco?" Joe asked.

"Since I learned my husband was killed in the war," she answered. So she was a war widow. *No short supply of them*, Joe mused to himself. The war made a lot of young widows. "I have to work to support my daughter. She's eight now."

Sam had lent him some money because he was broke. So he took out a ten-dollar bill and gave it to her. She smiled a beautiful smile and said, "Thank you so much. Now I can pay my rent."

In the meantime, in the corner of his eye, he saw that the money in front of Sam was getting bigger. He was obviously winning. But he saw a pile of money in the middle of the table that was growing even larger. Seemed like betting was really heavy. Maybe he had a really good hand or something. He turned back to talk to Betsy some more, and then he heard a shot ring out. He looked over and saw Sam holding a smoking Colt. He saw one gambler slumped in his chair with his gun still in his hand resting on the table. Sam was holding his six-gun on the other two. Joe immediately drew his Colt and walked over to help cover the two gamblers.

"Cheatin'," Sam was saying with disgust. "No deck has five aces. This money is mine, so I'm taking it."

Joe helped Sam keep the gamblers covered until Sam had scooped up all his money, then immediately ran out to get the horses. Sam had put the money in various pockets in his vest and coat and held his gun on the two gamblers as he backed out the door. Then he turned and ran to his waiting horse. Joe was mounted on his horse and was holding Sam's horse for him and had the two packhorses on a lead rope. So they rode out of town.

They kept their horses at a full gallop for about five miles or so, heading south across the snow-covered plains. Then they drew up to let the horses blow, and Joe and Sam both looked back to see if there were any signs of pursuit. He didn't know if anyone would follow or not. A lot of times, no one cared if you shot a gambler. It was only if the gambler had friends or not. And Sam didn't really know if the other two gamblers in the game were even friends of the dead one.

There was no sign of pursuit. So they moved on southward with their horses at a walk. It was still the middle of the afternoon. They hadn't really even had time to stop at the general store to buy supplies. Maybe they'd come to another town. They just rode on. They'd look for a place to camp when it got near nightfall.

Toward evening, they saw a plume of smoke in the distance—probably a campfire. So they headed for it. They just rode on up as if they had not a single care in the world. They didn't want to be mistaken for hostiles. Joe noticed two men. They looked toward them, and one of them was holding a rifle. The other kept his hand near his six-gun. Joe didn't blame them. You never knew if someone was friend or foe out here.

When they were close enough, Joe said, "Hello. The fire. We're riding friendly."

Jim recognized Joe by the sound of his voice and then he saw Sam. Joe recognized Jim at about the same time. "The lieutenant!" he said with emphasis. "Fancy meeting you out here!" He reined in his horse and dismounted as did Sam.

"Sergeant Williams," Jim said with enthusiasm, "and Corporal Blake." He grabbed Joe's hand and wrung it good and pounded him on the back before he turned to Sam and did the same. After they finally finished with shaking hands and back pounding, Jim turned toward Jack and said, "Jack Watkins." Then he nodded to his two old friends and said, "Joe and Sam." Jack had been a first sergeant during the war.

Jack gave both of them a big grin while he shook hands with their new guests. "Glad to meet you," Jack told them. "So you must have served in the same outfit as Jim."

"All the way from Brandy Station to Appomattox," Joe replied.

"We've got coffee brewed," Jim told them. "Unsaddle and put your horses over with ours."

So Joe and Sam were finally reunited with their friend after nearly two years. They knew Jim had come West. Then they'd never heard from him anymore. They unsaddled their mounts and pack-horses and led them out near Jim and Jack's horses and hobbled them. Back at the fire, the coffee was obviously very welcome, and they set out to cook supper.

The campfire lit up the dark night. Each man sat on a log. The fire got the front of their bodies warm. Occasionally, one of them would stand up and turn his back to the fire to let his back warm up a little.

"We're on our way to West Texas to go mustanging," Jim said.

"We just got in from South Carolina," Joe said. "And it was a long ride."

"I remember that ride," said Jim. "I made it a year and a half ago."

"Can you tell us more about these mustangs you've been talking about?" asked Joe.

"Thousands of wild mustangs over west of here," Jack said. "They don't belong to anyone. Just there for the taking."

"And we need horses," added Jim. "We can saddle break them ourselves. And any extra we get we can sell."

"The best time to go horse hunting is in the winter," Jack then added. "Riding jobs are scarce this time of year, but we can go wild-horse hunting. My crew went mustanging many times before the war. When our outfit needed horses for working cattle, that's where we'd go to get them. But the horse hunting grounds are in the middle of Indian country. So we'll probably have to deal with a few Indian fights."

Fighting had been Joe's and Sam's stock in trade for two years. The same was true for Jim. Jack had fought for four years. So the idea of Indian fighting didn't seem like something so very different from what they had been doing.

"The first thing we'll have to have is a cavvy of horses. We have to able to change to a fresh horse anytime we want," Jack told them.

"And we'll have to have enough grub to last us several months. I have a ranch a little west of here. We can use my horses, but we'll need money to buy grub with."

Joe was broke. Sam had not only the money from the sale of his farm but also his winnings from today's poker game, so he had plenty of money. Jack and Jim still had most of their summer's wages in their pocket.

"I just sold my farm in South Carolina a few months ago," Sam then said. "I can provide us with a grubstake. You can pay me back when we sell some mustangs."

CHAPTER 5

Mustangers

The next morning, they had a breakfast of bacon with biscuits and gravy, and of course, all the hot coffee they wanted. After breakfast, Joe and Sam packed their pipes and lit them, but Jim and Jack just rolled a cigarette apiece. Then they broke camp, packed all the pack saddles, saddled up their horses, and started through the snow toward Jack's ranch, which was to the southwest. They just walked their horses until noon and then stopped for a noon camp. They loosened the cinches on the saddles and tethered the horses. Joe and Sam started gathering wood while Jim and Jack started a fire, put on the coffee, and cooked up another bait of biscuits and bacon. Jack also made a pan of gravy.

After the noon meal, they repacked the pack saddles on the packhorses, tightened the cinches on the saddle horses, remounted, and continued their journey. They noticed the snow got to be less and less as they continued on southwestward. After two days' travel, the snow was completely gone.

"We're near my papa's ranch," mentioned Jack on their fourth day. "I'd like to go visit him."

"We can take time out to do so," Jim said. They looked back toward Joe and Sam. They both nodded.

So they turned their horses directly south, and after a few hours, they saw ranch buildings in the distance.

They rode to the corral and put their horses inside and unsaddled them. They made sure they had water, and Jack climbed up into

21

the loft of the barn and forked down some hay for them. Then he led them to the cookshack.

"Might as well get some coffee," he told them.

They walked in, and the cook was cooking supper. "Why, hello, Jack!" he exclaimed as soon as he saw him and held out his hand.

Jack took it and shook it vigorously. "Hello, Simon! It's good to see you!"

"These are my partners." And he introduced the three men with him.

"Is Pa around?" he asked.

"He's riding with the men out, checking the range. They rode off south this time. They'll be back in time for supper."

Supper would be another hour or two, so Jack reached for the pot of coffee simmering on the stove. Simon brought them four cups. China cups this time, not the steel cups you had at a chuck wagon.

Jack poured each of them a cup of coffee, and they sat down at the long table.

"How are things going here?" Jack asked, looking at Simon.

"We're getting along pretty good. Just finished our fall branding. Hal and the boys are out riding looking for any sign of rustling or such." Hal was Jack's pa's name. He patrolled his range often when they didn't have roundups or branding or anything in progress to keep them busy. He wanted to be sure nothing was going on that shouldn't be.

They heard the hoof beats when Hal and the crew rode up. They went out to greet them. Jack walked out to the corral and opened the gate and held it open so they could ride in without having to dismount.

Hal dismounted and said, "Hello, son! Glad you're back home!" He held out his hand to shake hands. After Hal and his crew unsaddled their mounts, Jack introduced him to his three partners. Then they walked back to the cookshack. Cookie had supper ready by then. They all sat at the table to eat, about a dozen men in all.

Hal normally just had his meals in the cookshack with the men. He'd been a widower these twenty years or so and didn't bother with cooking in the big house.

"So are you back home for the winter?" Hal asked. He suspected otherwise. Why else would he have three partners?

"Going mustanging. I need more horses."

"Yeah, I knew you needed more horses than you've got for that ranch of yours. I've been sending a cowpuncher over to your place every week or so to make sure everything's okay. Don't want any squatters to come along and think it's an abandoned ranch."

"I appreciate it, Pa," said Jack. "You and me have been mustanging a lot of times, haven't we?"

"Yep, and some of the best horses we've got came from those horse hunts."

They kept talking and filling each other in on recent events. When it got near bedtime, Hal nodded to Jim, Joe, and Sam, "Y'all can sleep in the bunkhouse if you like. We don't keep as many hands in the winter as we do in the summer, so we have enough spare bunks."

So all four men went out to the barn and got their bedrolls and brought them in. They just left their saddles, chaps and rifles lying there in the barn. Their rifles were in saddle boots that were fastened to their saddles. They came in and found three unused bunks and turned in. They were tired. They slept good.

At breakfast the next morning, Hal told Cory, his foreman, "I'm going to ride with Jack to his place today. Figure I'll help him get everything ready to leave for their horse hunt." Cory nodded and went with the men to the corral to get them lined out for the day's work.

Hal didn't go to war because he decided he was too old. But there weren't any cowboys available during the war, so he didn't get any branding done either.

Hal, Jack, and the rest of the mustangers saddled up and headed toward Jack's place. When they reached his ranch, they found a small one-room log cabin and a corral and barn. They put their horses inside the corral, and Jack climbed the ladder to the loft so he could fork down some hay to them. While he was doing that, Jim primed the pump and pumped them some water into the watering trough.

Jack had a stack of firewood, so there was no need to chop wood. He had a potbellied stove inside his shack. But the shack was too small for five men to fit in comfortably, so they built a campfire outside and got the coffee started. Then Hal, Jack, and Jim each rolled a smoke. Joe and Sam packed their pipes and lit them. After everyone had a cup of coffee and a smoke, they started supper. Jim still had plenty of meat left from the maverick yearling he had killed a couple of days previously. So they decided to have boiled cow and potatoes with beans, biscuits, and gravy. And when they started eating, it really tasted good.

Jack told them, "I decided I wanted a spread of my own, so I started this place before the war. But no branding took place during the war, so they're all mavericks unless somebody else managed to slap their brand on some of them. But I do need more horses. We have enough for now to handle some mustanging."

After they ate, Jack heated some water on the stove to wash dishes. Joe and Sam volunteered to do the dishes as usual. After that, they sat around the fire, and Joe got out his mouth harp. He started playing. Jim had his mouth harp in his saddlebags. He quickly went and got it, came back to the fire, and started playing harmony to Joe. On some of the songs, he'd stop playing his harp and sing instead. They really enjoyed the cool night air and the good music. Hal wasn't used to music at the campfire, and you could see his appreciation in the way his eyes lit up.

They played and sang until they were tired. Jim and Jack were accustomed to sleeping outside. Both had been cowboying all summer. Jack's cabin had two bunks. So Jack suggested that Joe or Sam one take one of the two bunks. Hal would take one of them. Jack and Jim unrolled their bedrolls outside. Joe and Sam both decided to just sleep outside too.

CHAPTER 6

Starting Out

At the first ray of light the following morning, Jim and Jack both rolled out of their blankets, put on their hats, and pulled on their boots as if they were supposed to or something. They were accustomed to getting up at dawn. Jim stoked up the fire, and Jack put the coffeepot on. Joe and Sam woke up to the smell of coffee perking. They stomped into their boots and stumbled over to the fire, sleepy-eyed. Hal apparently smelled the coffee too, because he came walking out of the cabin at about that time.

Joe remarked, "That there sun ain't even up yet."

"This is what time cowboys get up," Jim said. "And mustangers too."

For breakfast, they had biscuits and bacon and gravy again and all the hot coffee they wanted. Then they each rolled a smoke and lit it. Joe and Sam did the dishes again. They didn't have cigarettes back east. That's why Joe and Sam both smoked their pipes. They packed their pipes and lit them so they could get a smoke too. They puffed their pipes a few minutes before they started the dishes. They had metal plates and cups as a chuck wagon would use. Jim and Jack had done the cooking as before. Jack explained to them that they needed to go find his horse cavvy and round them up and bring them in. They'd have to have their cavvy of horses before they did anything else. They had to have a string of at least eight or ten horses for each man. So they wanted to have a minimum of at least forty horses in their cavvy.

So after they put out the campfire, they went out to the corral, saddled up, and went searching for Jack's horses. "They've been ranging over to the southwest of here," Hal told them. "My puncher rides until he finds the horses every time he comes over checking on things. That's usually where they're at."

Jack explained that he had a stallion and about twenty or so broodmares with colts and about forty or so geldings. The colts would be weaned by now. "We'll leave the mares and colts and just take the geldings," he said. "Except for a couple of mares. Geldings are more contented if you have a mare or two in the herd."

They found the horses at about midmorning and ran them in. The broodmares, stallion, and colts were running in a separate herd. The stallion kept the mares and colts separate from the geldings. So they just left them where they were except for two old mares that Jack picked out. Then they gathered up the geldings and the two mares and headed them for the corral.

Jack rode ahead to open the corral gate and make sure the seven horses they'd left in the corral didn't get out. They ran the horses in. After they closed the gate, one of the mares came up to Jack and nuzzled his pocket. He pulled out a biscuit and fed it to her. She was apparently a pet.

Then they put the pack saddles on the packhorses and loaded them up with grub and supplies. And Jack put several old lariat ropes in with the gear being packed on one of the packhorses. When a cowboy bought a new rope, he didn't throw away the old one. He'd put it somewhere in the barn in case he needed it for lead ropes and such at some later time. And Jack knew they'd need more lead ropes where they were going.

Jack opened the gate to let the horses out, and they started them in a westward direction where Jack knew they'd find some good mustang stock. Hal was sitting his horse as they rode off and waved to them as they left.

"It will probably be several weeks before we reach mustang country," Jack remarked as they rode along. The brush was thick. There was still some soapweed and cactus around but also a lot of mesquite bushes. There were clumps of mesquite so thick you couldn't ride through them. Any part of the ground that wasn't covered in brush was covered with grass. The grass was still green in spite of the late season. They had removed the hackamores from the packhorses and just let them herd with the horse herd during the day while traveling. Jim and Jack both carried ropes on their saddles. They figured they would just rope the packhorses and bring them in when they made camp before they unsaddled them.

At noon, they stopped near a creek, and Jack let the horses drink. After they finished drinking, they started grazing. He continued his role as wrangler while the other three men started making their noon camp. Jim had roped the packhorse that was carrying their grub and brought him up to the fire. They removed his pack and then turned him loose to graze with the other horses. While Joe and Sam were unpacking what they needed, Jim roped the other packhorse and brought him in to the fire to take off his pack. Then he turned him loose to graze too. That packhorse wasn't carrying any grub, just the supplies they knew they'd need.

Since Jack was doing the wrangling, the other three men started gathering up brush to make a fire. They found there was plenty of dead mesquite brush lying around. After they had a fire going, Jim put the coffee on, and then Joe and Sam helped him cook some bacon and biscuits and gravy.

After they had eaten, Jim went out to relieve Jack of his duties of herding the horse cavvy so he could come in and eat. Then they put out the fire, tightened their cinches, washed and packed up the plates, cups, and skillets, and then put the pack saddles on the packhorses again. They got the horse herd bunched up. Then they resumed their journey. They continued to spot wild cattle in the distance on their way. Then they saw a blackened heap ahead of them. When they got closer, they could see that it was the remains of a burned-out cabin and barn.

"Used to be a homestead," Jack mused as they rode up. "The frontier has been pushed back eastward several hundred miles due to the war. There simply weren't enough soldiers to prevent the predations of the hostile Indians. But," he further explained, "that is to our advantage as far as our horse hunt is concerned. Wild mustangs will be found only in Indian country. Otherwise, they'd already belong to someone else. So once we reach a place where we can gather up a herd of wild horses, we'll have to be on guard for an Indian attack at all times."

This made sense to Jim. Joe and Sam had gone through two years of war with Jim. They were experienced soldiers, though they weren't experienced Indian fighters yet. At night, when they camped, they kept four horses saddled and tied near camp, and they took turns on night guard with the horse herd. They didn't really expect any raids from Indians yet. They weren't far enough west. But horse thieves might be prowling about.

Each morning, they cooked a breakfast of biscuits and gravy and some kind of meat. And they were about to run low on meat. Jack had decided that someone should scout ahead just to make sure there was no one laying for them. So Jack and Jim took turns scouting and horse wrangling. Joe and Sam could handle horse wrangling okay too. Both of them had spent two years in the cavalry, so they were plenty experienced with horses, though neither of them knew how to rope.

They came to a place where the grass was especially good and decided to let the horses rest a couple of days. "You and Sam need to learn how to rope," Jack told Joe. So he took his rope and shook out a loop. He tossed the loop at a soapweed bush about forty feet away. It circled around the bush with no problem.

He coiled up the rope and handed it to Joe. "Now you try it," Jack told him. He did and missed it by about ten feet.

"Harder than it looks," said Joe.

"Yep. Try again."

Jack took two spare ropes from one of the packs of the packhorses and handed one to Joe and the other to Sam. When they decided to gather some dead wood for the fire, Jack took his rope and mounted up. He shook out a loop and roped a dead mesquite limb. Then he dragged it up to camp. Joe and Sam saw what he was doing, mounted their horses, and did likewise. It looked like a good way to practice roping from the saddle, and they could pull up wood for the fire at the same time.

After a couple of days, they packed the pack saddles onto the packhorses and resumed their journey. After about two weeks, they came to what would be the last settlement before the frontier. And it wasn't much. It was not really a town—just a general store and two saloons. But they noticed there was a sign in front of the general store that said Menard. So the store had a name. It catered mostly to buffalo hunters and roving cowpokes. But when they stopped at the general store to replenish their supplies, Sam gave Jack the money he'd need to buy food and supplies with. Jack had a tally book that he used to keep a record of all the brands near his ranch. So he got it out and wrote down the date and the amount of purchase so they could keep track of it.

"We'll reimburse you before we compute any profits," Jack told him. "And you'll get a share of the profits too." While they were in the store, Sam bought two hemp ropes—one for himself and one for Joe. They both wanted a new rope. An old rope wasn't strong enough and might break when you least expected it. And Jack bought four shovels and a small crosscut saw. It had a handle made of wood that was shaped like a rectangle except with the ends leaning out a little bit where they joined the saw blade. One man could saw with it, but it could also be used by two men.

Sam noticed a saloon across the street when they stopped at the general store. "We got time to wet our whistle?" he asked.

"If we did, you'd probably get in a card game and shoot somebody," Joe said. "We'd be better off to not mix business with pleasure."

"I sure am thirsty," Sam complained.

"We bought plenty of coffee. Besides, we have to watch the horse herd."

Jim had stayed with the cavvy to keep them bunched up while the others were buying supplies. Jack went out and rounded up the packhorses and brought them in to load their supplies. He roped each one and put a hackamore on him first. They loaded up their supplies on their packhorses and were ready to start. But Jim noticed they only had three riders. He looked around to see who was missing. Sam was gone.

CHAPTER 7

Sam Is Missing

"Where is Sam?" Jim asked to no one in particular.

Everyone looked around. They hadn't noticed they had a man missing until now.

"I don't know where he's at, but I know where to look," said Joe.

"And where is that?" asked Jack.

"Probably the saloon. I'll go get him."

Joe turned his horse back toward the little town. Jack said to Jim, "I'll go with him."

Jim said, "I'll go too. The horses are grazing. They'll be all right for a few minutes."

They rode over to the saloon that was right across the general store. Joe figured that was probably the saloon where they'd find Sam. If not, they would go to the other one. There were two.

They went through the swinging doors and walked in. They just went on walking past the bar and toward a back room. And sure enough, Sam was setting there with a handful of cards in front of him, and there was money in the middle of the table.

"I'll cover your ten and bet ten more," Sam said.

"We have to leave," Joe told Sam.

"I want to play just one game," Sam answered.

"You'll turn in your cards after you finish this hand!" Joe ordered.

"But I'm feeling lucky!" Sam insisted.

Then they heard gunshots coming from outside and the thunder of horses' hooves. "Someone's stealing our horses!" Jack yelled and turned and ran toward the door. Jim and Joe were right behind him. They mounted their horses quickly and headed toward the stampeding horses.

Jim pulled his six-gun and leaned forward with his cheek on his horse's neck. The horses were already running madly across the prairie toward the northeast. Jim tried to find a target to shoot at, but the dust of the running horses obscured his view. But all three riders continued their pursuit.

Jim looked ahead and saw a cluster of boulders very near their path. He was on the right of the other two riders. He swerved toward Jack and pointed to the left. Jack had no choice but to follow him because his horse crowded up against Jack's horse. Joe made the turn too to keep from being run over by Jack. They raced to a cluster of trees near a dry creek bottom. When they neared the trees, Jim started reining in his horse and held up his arm to get the others to do so too.

"Dry gulcher at that cluster of boulders," he breathed.

"How do you know that?" Jack asked.

"Just a likely place for him to be. We'll skirt way around him and keep following after the horses."

Just before they reached the clump of trees, Jack saw a glint of sunlight from a rifle barrel in the middle of the cluster of boulders. "There's a dry gulcher there all right," he then said.

So the three riders skirted way around to the north keeping out of range of the cluster of boulders. In the corner of his eye, Jack saw a rider rushing toward them. He recognized Sam's gray. So Sam had caught up with them.

The rustlers had turned right when they passed the dried creek bed. They apparently saw their pursuers make their detour. Jim looked toward the right and saw a small amount of dust rising just on the other side of the trees along the dried creek bed. So the dry gulcher had left his nest and was riding toward the fleeing horse herd.

The dried creek bed continued to wind around to the right until they were heading south. And Jim figured out the sniper's strategy. While they went around outside the creek bed, he had cut across and was ahead of them again. He yelled at the other men, "Stop a minute!" They pulled their horses to a stop. The horses obviously wanted to run. It was hard to hold them still. "I'm going into the woods to find the dry gulcher. If you get near there, he'll get a shot at you. Don't ride after the horses just yet. Wait here at the creek bed, and if he comes out, you can get him."

"I'll go with you," Jack said. "I'll ride around the other side of the trees from where he's at and watch for him on the other side."

"Okay, but we'd have to be careful who we shoot at then. You couldn't just shoot at a glint on a rifle barrel. You might shoot me."

"I'll make sure I identify my target first before I shoot. You'll have to do the same."

Jim and Jack both rode back the direction they came from. They worked around the wooded area where it appeared the sniper had gone. Jack halted and tied his horse to a tree. He told Jim, "This is where I'll be." Jim rode on.

When he reached a place where the trees were thicker, Jim holstered his six-gun and pulled his horse to a halt. He rode on up to the first tree, dismounted, and tied his horse to it. He pulled his rifle out of the saddle boot and walked into the woods. This was the likeliest place for the unknown rifleman to make another try, but now Jim was stalking him.

He kept creeping through the woods as quietly as he could and tried to think of where the best place for a rifleman to make a stand would be. Then he halted. He felt a tingling between his shoulder blades. He dived forward and hit the ground just as a shotgun blast went off above him! A shotgun! Not a rifle! So the dry gulcher was waiting in the boulders for them with a shotgun! Jim rolled over and fired at the spot that the shotgun blast had come from. Then he scooted forward enough to get himself behind a tree and looked on both sides of the tree to see if he could see him. Nope. No sign of him. He listened. There were no sounds except for the bristle of wind in the trees. He figured whoever moved first would be the one to die, so he just held his position and kept as still as he could. There was still no sign of movement.

There was no sound of birds singing—no sound at all except the light bustle of wind in the trees. Jim looked all around to see if he could detect any movement anywhere. There was nothing but the light movement of the leaves in the tops of the trees. It took patience to just sit and do nothing and just be as still as possible.

In spite of it being wintertime, it got hot. South Texas has some hot days in the middle of the winter. There was still no sign of movement. Then Jim heard a rustle of leaves to his left. He looked over toward it and brought his rifle in position. It was a javelina pig. But something must have spooked him. Jim just held his position and remained as quiet as possible. Then it occurred to him to look behind him! He rolled over, and there was a man leveling his shotgun at him! Jim shot him and levered in another shell. The man fell.

Jim got up and walked over to him. He was dead. There was nothing unusual about him. He was wearing a black hat, tan shirt, black vest, and pants with boots and spurs. He was dressed like a cowboy would dress.

He heard a rustle of leaves to his right. "It's okay, Jack. I got him," he said. He wanted Jack to hear his voice so he wouldn't shoot at him.

Jack walked up. "Looks like he was using a Greener," Jack mused.

"Yeah. He was depending on getting a close-up shot at us."

Jack went to his horse as did Jim. They mounted and rode to where they had left Joe and Sam. They resumed following the tracks of the horse herd. After an hour or so, they saw the horses in the distance. The horses had run themselves out and had halted and were breathing heavily. All four of the pursuers drew their six-guns and started looking for a target to shoot at. Nothing. There was nothing there but the herd of exhausted horses.

So they rode around them very carefully and got them headed west again. There was no sign of the horse thieves.

"Apparently they counted on the dry gulcher taking us out while were we chasing them. When their ruse failed, they cleared out," Jim said.

"Yes, that is how it appears," Jack said.

They kept the horses moving at a slow walk and kept an eye on their back trail. Jim checked the two packhorses and found that one of them had lost his pack and the other one's pack had slipped down under his belly. Jim dismounted and fixed his pack saddle. They had to drive the horses back near the store and go in and replenish their supplies again. Sam sheepishly gave Jack the money he needed to pay for them.

Then they headed their horse herd back to the west again.

CHAPTER 8

A Mustang Trap

Three days later, in the middle of the afternoon, they came upon a buffalo herd.

"We're low on camp meat," Jim mused when he saw the buffalo.

"Yep," said Jack and pulled his rifle out of the saddle boot.

They rode over close enough to the buffalo herd to be in range and Jack shot a weaning-sized calf. The other buffalo didn't seem to notice the one fallen calf. It had already been weaned, so its mother wasn't nearby. But when they rode up to the dead calf, the herd started moving off.

They dismounted, and Jim helped Jack field dress the buffalo and skin it out. Then they cut it into four quarters. Jack rolled up two of the quarters inside the hide and tied it behind his saddle. Jim put each of the other two quarters in a flour sack each and tied them behind his saddle

"Let's stop and make camp now and cook some fresh meat," Jack suggested. "It's time to let the horses get some rest anyway."

They had just crossed a creek a couple of miles previously, so they turned the horses around and moved them back to the creek and made camp. Jack had wrapped the liver inside the hide with the meat.

After they got the campfire going, Jack asked, "Anybody that don't like fresh liver?" You never knew if you didn't ask.

"Fine with me," Sam said.

"I do like liver," Joe then said.

Jim just nodded. So Jack sliced up the liver and got it frying in a pan while Sam and Joe peeled some potatoes and got them frying. They had some leftover bacon grease. When they fried bacon, they put the grease in a can with a piece of rawhide for a lid. The lid was fastened on with a rawhide string. They had themselves a gourmet meal that night.

They let the horses rest for two days before they broke camp and saddled up again. As they moved on westward, they did see some wild cattle in the distance, but the cow critters seemed to ignore them. One time, when riding over a rise, they came upon some wild longhorns. They looked up, snorted, and stampeded. So they apparently couldn't get close to them without getting them riled.

After about three weeks from the beginning of their trip, they started seeing more herds of mustangs. Once, when they peaked out on a rise, they saw some mustangs that looked like they were about a mile off. They spooked and ran instantly upon sight of them. So they were even spookier than the cattle.

They found a good place near a creek to pitch camp.

"This camping spot should be easily defended," Jack said. "We're in Indian country now, so we need a place to herd the horses into to make them harder to steal. If Indians learn we are camped here, the first thing they'll probably do will be to try to steal them."

One advantage they had was the fact that it was the middle of the winter. Indians didn't normally go on the warpath during the winter. If the Indians ran low on meat, they would take a hunting party out in search of buffalo. But otherwise, they weren't likely to have to deal with an Indian attack until spring. Now a hunting party of Indians might spot them and decide to make an exception. So it was better to be safe than sorry. And it wasn't very cold this far south. They weren't sure the Indians weren't moving about.

Over the camp fire, Jack started explaining what they'd need to do to build a mustang trap. "We need to build some wide wings out of brush so the horses won't suspect it's manmade but will funnel the horses toward the corral. There will be the remains of a trap from the last time I went mustang hunting near here. I trapped horses here several times before the war."

Cowboys don't like to work off the back of a horse. And that was true of both Jack and Jim though they'd make an exception at a time like now. Joe and Sam, both being farmers, were accustomed to working on foot.

The next morning, they started building their trap. They rode to Jack's old trap, which was nothing but rotten posts by now. So they had to fell some trees just the right size, trim the branches off them, and then drag them to where they'd build their trap. They fastened a rope to one end of each log and the other to the saddle horn to drag them up. Jack got his saw out, and they sawed them into posts and rails.

"The purpose of this trap is to capture a whole drove of mustangs at a time. We'll build the pen behind that clump of trees right there. They won't see the corral fence until they're inside. The pen will be shaped in a circle so that the trapped mustangs can't rush into a corner and break the fence." They took the shovels that Jack had bought at the last town, and after digging up the old rotten posts, they dug a hole where each post was to be. Then they placed the posts upright in the holes and then tamped the dirt in thoroughly around the posts. They lashed the rails and posts together at the top with strong rawhide thongs. Then they put two more rails in the middle. The rawhide from Jim's maverick came in handy at this point. They cut it into strips and used it to lash the rails to the posts. They had saved the buffalo hide, but Jack knew it wasn't cured enough to work yet. When they were done, they had a fence that was somewhat elastic and hard to break. Jack had unrolled the buffalo hide and staked it out so it could start curing.

Next in order were the wings, which went out from either side of the gate, forming an immense V, with the gate of the pen at the apex. The wing fences were made of brush and treetops, which meant they had to go fell some more trees. The longer wing was half a mile or more in length, the other about half as long. Then came the gate.

The gate was made to be closed with bars. They had cut notches in the posts for the gate so they could just drop a rail into each notch about two feet apart on each post. "Two rails will be enough. We'll put a blanket over it. The horses won't go near it," Jack explained.

When they had finished with the pen and the wings, Jack showed them how to cut green brush and use it to cover all evidences of any manmade structures. It was wintertime, but there were evergreen bushes everywhere that they could use.

"If the mustangs see any evidence of manmade doings at the trap, they'll never come near it," Jack told them.

They went back to camp, which was downwind from their trap. The prevailing wind was from the southwest, so their camp was about a mile or so to the northeast. Jack had thought of everything. Joe and Sam had each roped a clump of brush and drug it up to camp. Jim and Jack unpacked the packhorses and turned them loose with the horse herd. They had managed to find a campsite that was in a draw with thick brush on three sides. So it would be harder for the Indians to stampede the horses if they tried to steal them.

Jack and Jim spent some time scouting around, looking for Indian sign while Joe and Sam were cooking supper. Supper was buffalo hump steak, fried potatoes, biscuits and gravy, and of course, hot coffee. Each man was well-fed when he rolled a cigarette and lit it.

Instead of lighting his pipe, Joe said, "I'd like to try out one of those cigarettes." He watched Jim roll one, then Jim handed him the tobacco sack and one of the papers. Joe's first attempt was a flop. Jim rolled him one and handed it to him. He lit it and took a drag from it. "It does taste good," Joe concluded.

Sam had watched Jim roll his cigarette and saw Joe roll the one that didn't work. When he tried it, he actually had a cigarette he could light. The tobacco they used for cigarettes was better-tasting tobacco than what they had for their pipes. No wonder Jack and Jim just rolled cigarettes instead of taking the time with a pipe.

"Tomorrow, we'll go looking for mustangs," Jack told them over the campfire that night. "I don't know if we'll run any of them, but we need to find out where they are. So we'll mainly just be scouting the area."

Running Mustangs

"I think we'd better post a watch on the horses tonight," Jack told them before it was time to turn in. "We haven't seen any Indian sign yet, but they still might show up by surprise."

"I agree," Sam said. "And I'll take the first watch."

"I'll take the second watch," Joe then said.

It turned out that Jim had the last watch before dawn. When Jim saw barely a trace of gray in the east, he rode into camp and dismounted. He tied his horse to a bush and then started the fire. Then he went and touched each of the others lightly on the shoulder. That was all it took to wake up a cowboy.

Jim put the coffee on while the other men rolled up their bedrolls. Then he started slicing up bacon and placing the pieces in a skillet to fry. Sam put some flour and baking powder in a bowl and started the biscuit batter.

After breakfast, Jim took his horse and rode out to the cavvy to rope a horse for each of the other men. He brought them in one at a time. They saddled up and started out. Sam stayed behind to wash up the pots and pans and keep an eye on the horse cavvy.

"We'll spread out so there is about thirty to forty yards between us," Jack whispered to them. "Then we'll ride northeast."

They didn't see any mustangs, but they did come up over a rise and flushed a small herd of wild longhorns. They had plenty of camp meat and weren't looking for longhorns, so they ignored the stampeding cattle and kept riding.

They rode till noon but still didn't see any mustangs. They rode back to camp. When they arrived back in camp, they found that Sam was still out herding the horses. They dismounted and started cutting wood for the fire.

After they had dinner, they roped fresh horses and headed to the northwest. Then after about ten miles or so, they turned to the right and started making a big circle around their new trap. They were careful to stop at each rise and ride up slowly, just peeking over the top to see if they saw any mustangs before going farther.

"We don't want to run any mustangs yet," Jack commented. "We just want to find out where they are."

They did spot several small droves of mustangs and wild cattle too. They noted that the cattle all herded separately from the mustangs. The mustang mares maintained small herds, with a stallion watching over each herd. They also saw occasional bachelor herds: herds of stallions that hadn't managed to whip off a stallion and get a herd of mares of their own. When they got a good look over a stretch of flat plains, and if they hadn't been seen by the wild critters, they retraced their path and rode on further around their circle, then stopped, approached some ridge, and repeated the process.

When they arrived back in camp that night, Jack said, "We can possibly run some mustangs in the morning. If we run the horse cavvy into that boxed canyon nearby, it'll probably be okay to leave them alone till noon or so. The plan is for the four of us to find a likely herd of mustangs and approach them and spread out with a line of four riders, about twenty-five yards or so between each rider at first. Then, once we have them headed for the trap, we'll spread out, and Jim and me will really push our ponies and strive to reach the outer wings of the trap at the same time as the herd. That way, we can hopefully turn them if it looks like they are going to try to go around the trap.

"Joe and Sam, once we start the mustangs to running, you'll spread out so you're about a hundred yards or so apart and continue to ride and yell and wave your hats or ropes or whatever and keep them moving into the trap. I'll take the shorter wing on the east end.

When they are inside the trap, whoever's closest to the gate will put two bars across it and place a blanket over them."

They had spotted a herd about fifteen miles or so to the north of the trap the previous day. They were up before dawn. It was pitch-black when they started the fire. They finished breakfast and saddled up. The horse cavvy was in the box canyon grazing and was near water. They got their camp water from a nearby creek; and the creek ran through the box canyon where they left the horses, so Jack still figured the horses would be okay by themselves for a few hours.

It was midmorning by the time they had maneuvered into position north of where the herd of mustangs was believed to be. Then all four of them rode over the ridge and found the mustang drove right where they expected. They just started riding toward them slowly. The stallion looked up and saw them first and immediately nipped a couple of mares in the rump and got them moving. They stampeded toward the south just as the men intended. But after about ten miles of hard riding, the mustang stallion turned his herd and drove them to the east. The four men rode as hard as they could to turn them, but there was no use. You can't outrun a mustang. For one thing, their horses were all mounted, and the mustangs weren't encumbered with riders. But the mustangs started their run completely fresh too, and the four mustangers had been riding for a few hours already.

"There will be another day," Jack said as he pulled his horse to a walk.

That afternoon, they rode toward camp looking for another possible herd of wild ones. They flushed a herd of bachelor broncs by surprise while riding over a rise. But instead of running toward the trap, they started running the opposite direction. When a mustang decides which direction he is going to run, he'll run that direction regardless of any hazing or hat-waving the riders might do. So there was nothing they could do but just go looking for another bunch.

The four riders fanned out and started moving slowly southward toward the trap looking for horse critters. When just topping a rise, they saw a bunch in the distance. They saw the stallion look up and sniff the air. He started his bunch of mares moving but to the west instead of the south. They were out of sight by the time the riders reached the point where the mustangs were when they saw them.

They were within about five miles or so of their trap by this time. They flushed another bunch of mares with a red stallion, but they ran the wrong way too. It was turning out to be a frustrating day.

When they neared their camp, they decided to ride into camp and cook something to eat. It was nearly noon. After they had their meal of buffalo meat, biscuits, and beans, Jack said they probably should try riding west maybe. The mustangs they saw to the north would make a big circle and come back to where they started from in a few days. And they had no idea of a trap nearby, so they could be run again. He explained how you can't expect them to run the same direction each day, but whatever direction they did run, they would normally circle back to their original location in a few days.

They made a big semicircle to the south and made their way to a spot about twenty miles or so west of their trap. Then they spread out and started looking for bunches of mustangs again.

It wasn't long before they spotted another bunch. They were at least a mile off. They were spotted by the bunch at the same time, and the wild ones started running. The four men just followed them in an easy lope, not hurrying. After they were about three or four miles from the trap, Jack motioned them to slant over to the south. Jim saw his logic. If the mustangs thought you wanted them to run north, they'd probably run south instead. And the trap was to the south of where they were running. And the mustangs did turn to the south right toward the trap. By then, they could see that it was a herd of bachelor stallions.

They gave chase. They still had them running toward the trap, so they kept them moving. The herd of mustangs ran right into the trap. Jack made it to the shorter wing on the north just as the mustangs came even with it. Jim was already moving down the longer wing, making sure they didn't get a chance to turn. But the mustangs just kept on stampeding until they got past the gate. Jack dismounted and got two bars over the gate and draped a blanket across it. So they had their first bunch in the trap!

The other three riders rode up, and Jim counted the heads of the circling horses. They were still racing around the circular pen looking for a way out, but he was able to count them—forty-three head.

"Not bad for a first catch," Jack told them.

Another Bunch

Their first task with their herd of wild horses was to geld and brand them, then to herd break them. But they turned the scrubs loose first. They wouldn't waste time with them. They turned loose nine of them. A couple of them had legs too short; several were too old. Three of them were paints. They didn't want the paint horses even if they were good horses. A cowboy might get mistaken for an Indian on a dark night. So they turned them out too. But they wound up with thirty-four really good horses in all out of the bunch.

"We'll brand and geld these before we do anything else," Jack told them. "Then we'll herd break them."

Jack started the fire. They'd have to use a running iron for the branding since there was no blacksmith shop available to use to make branding irons.

"We need to decide on a brand," Jack said. "My brand is the Rolling JW. We can decide on a new brand for our bunch. We'll register it when we get back to civilization. We can assume the brand 4 bar C. It could stand for the 4 Cavaliers."

Jack built a fire just inside the horse corral and got two running irons started on heating. Then Jim or Jack roped one of the gelding's front legs, throwing him, tied his legs securely with piggin' string, then Joe brought them a hot branding iron. Jack put a 4 bar C brand on the left side of the neck of the mustang, and Jim had his knife out ready to geld him. After Jack branded each bronc and Jim made him into a gelding, Jack tied his right front leg to his left hind foot before letting him up.

They repeated this process for all the stallions in the herd. It took them two days of hard work.

"We can herd break them now," Jack said. "They can't run with a front foot tied to a back foot, but they can walk around okay and graze. And they need water, so we'll take them to the creek to drink." There was no water inside the corral. Jack knew it would be okay to let them go a couple of days without water, but they'd need water after that. They had also been several days without eating, so they also needed to graze. The needs of nature keeping them preoccupied with water and feed served as a distraction that helped make the herd-breaking easier.

They waited another day before turning them out with the horse cavvy. They needed water and grass, but Jack wanted to give them time to settle down from the branding and gelding.

Jack explained, "They'll still break from the herd if they can as long as they're near their home grazing grounds. We'll have to keep them hobbled."

Jim was really glad they had brought Jack along. He was learning a lot of new things, and while Joe and Sam were willing workers, they hadn't really even perfected their roping yet. Sam was a good cook and was always willing to do the cooking. And Joe and Sam both were hard workers.

They turned the horses out and let them join the cavvy. After that, they then went out in search of another bunch. Jack had cautioned them to take the thongs off their six-shooters as soon they reached a point where they might be able to flush a herd of wild ones. They found another drove of mares with a really nice-looking stallion and started them running. But the stallion apparently sensed what they wanted him to do and started his herd north instead of south. They just ran right through the four riders and would have run over them if they hadn't gotten out of the way. There was nothing they could do but to let them go. It wasn't really a surprise. That was what they had experienced over and over. Wild horses didn't drive the direction you wanted them to go. They continued their search for another unsuspecting herd of wild ones.

They came upon another herd of mares with a black stallion. The black stallion snorted and turned and faced them with hate in his eyes. He immediately charged the closest rider he saw, which was Jack. Jack yanked out his six-shooter and shot him between the eyes; there was nothing else he could do. He would have killed his horse if he had succeeded in getting his teeth in his neck. The mares scattered immediately and ran all different directions.

Later that day, when they rode over a rise, they surprised another herd. It was a chestnut stallion with about a dozen mares and as many half-grown colts. Joe was the closest rider, and the stud did get his teeth in the neck of Joe's horse. He ripped his neck open, and the poor, dying horse made a half somersault, of course, unseating his rider. Then the horse headed for Joe and would have killed him if Jim hadn't managed to get his six-gun out and shoot the stallion just behind the ear. The studhorse died instantly, and the mares scattered, which could be expected. Jim took his six-gun and took the time to put Joe's horse out of his misery. He let Joe get up behind him to ride back to camp, and Jack brought along his saddle and bridle. He tied the saddle behind his saddle pommel up.

It was three days later before they finally found a herd of mares and a bay stallion and managed to get them stampeded in the right direction. They got them headed straight for the trap. They were about two hours' distance from the trap at the time they started their run. Their horses were covered with lather, and their sides were heaving by the time that Jack got the two bars up with the blanket draped over it. No way they'd come near the entrance once the blanket was there.

This time, the count was forty-two mares, thirty-eight weaned colts, and a stallion. Their first task was to throw and geld the stallion. And an impossible task it turned out to be. Their plan was to get two ropes on his neck and then Jack would rope his front feet and throw him. But as soon as they got their three roping horses inside the pen, he charged them with a look of pure hatred. He went straight for Jack, and he wasn't after his horse. If his massive jaws closed on Jack's leg, he wouldn't have much leg left. Jack had no choice but to grab his six-gun and shoot him between the eyes. He maneuvered his horse out of the way just in time as the giant stallion turned half a somersault and sprawled on the ground.

"How are we going to collect a herd of mustangs if you keep shooting them?" chided Jim.

"Yeah, we do have one less now, don't we?" answered Jack.

Jack put a rope around his neck as did Jim, and they drug him out of the pen. Sam dismounted and opened the gate and then closed it again after they had him free of the pen. They dragged him on over a rise and into a draw. Jim and Joe rode to camp to get the shovels and came back and covered him with dirt.

But they had their first herd of mares.

*****

He Who Rides Fast was hidden behind a rock in a saddle between two hills. And he saw wild horses being chased by four white men mounted on fast horses. "White men. Stealing Indian ponies," he murmured to himself. The Apache considered all wild horses on their hunting grounds to be Indian horses. He watched them ride on past and then he turned and walked down the hill to his waiting mount. He mounted and headed back to the village. He would report this theft to the tribe elders immediately!

It was winter, but the weather was warm. Southwest Texas frequently has warm weather during the winter. This would be an opportunity to count coup and add to his own string of war ponies. He rode quickly to the village and rode directly to the lodge of his uncle, Big Wolf. He told his uncle what he saw. "I saw white men stealing Apache horses!"

Big Wolf only paused a few seconds, then said, "Come with me."

They immediately went to the lodge of one of the elders. After He Who Rides Fast recounted again to the elder what he saw, all three of them went to the chief's lodge and notified him.

The chief told them, "Call a war council."

47

White men stealing Indian ponies! This was something they could not allow! So the three Apaches walked around the village letting all the elders know that the chief had called a council of the tribal elders to take place that afternoon.

They met in the wigwam of the chief. He Who Rides Fast was invited to the council meeting. They went through the ritual of smoking their peace pipe. Each Apache took a puff of the pipe and then blew the smoke upward. Some of them blew smoke rings.

After the peace pipe had gone around the full circle of braves and elders, the chief asked He Who Rides Fast to tell them about what he saw.

"I saw four white men on horseback stealing Apache ponies," he explained. "They had a large herd of horses they were driving to the south."

"Who will speak?" the chief then said after He Who Rides Fast was finished.

Lone Wolf looked up, which was a sign he wanted to speak. The chief nodded to him. "When the white men come, they take the best horses. They turn the worst horses loose. And they come again and again. We must stop them."

Three other elders wanted to speak and be recognized. They all agreed that the white thieves must be stopped. So the chief decided to plan a raid against the white men and reclaim all the horses that had been stolen and probably take some scalps in the bargain. So the chief decided to have a war dance that night.

Their drums could be heard well into the night.

*****

The next morning, after the mustangers had succeeded in capturing the herd of mares, Jack thought they should scout the area to make sure there were no Indians about. They didn't raid as much during the winter, but the weather had been warm. And that was the very thing that would encourage the Indians to prowl.

So Jack and Jim both rode off in opposite directions looking for Indian sign while Joe and Sam remained in camp to watch over their horses. They were both back by noon. Jack dismounted and filled them in on what he had seen. "Moccasin tracks. Over to the west. There were also tracks of an unshod horse, so an Indian apparently had dismounted and walked up a hill to observe while we brought in that last drove of wild horses."

Jim had returned from his scout to the east with nothing to report. "Sure, I saw lots of tracks of unshod horses, but mustangs would always be unshod unless they had once been domesticated and ran wild later. But I didn't see any Indian sign especially."

"Let's herd the horses back into the box canyon where we were keeping them while out searching for mustangs. That would make it more difficult to steal them," Jack suggested.

CHAPTER 11

Apache Attack

They moved their camp to the head of the canyon to some rocks that would be more easily defended. Then, with Joe left behind to watch over their herd, they went back to the trap and threw each mare and foal and tied a front foot to a back foot so they couldn't escape. Then they ran them out of the trap and herded them into the box canyon too. They wanted more mustangs, but they needed to finish herd breaking the ones they had first.

So Joe stayed behind to guard the horses while Jim, Jack, and Sam went to patrol the area from all approaches to their canyon. It would be better if they could avoid a surprise. They rode together in case they happened to come upon Indians. They'd have a better chance if there were three of them.

They rode to the northwest to the place where Jack had found Indian sign. They noted the direction indicated by the tracks of the pony where the moccasin tracks disappeared. "Apaches, I expect," Jack told them. They followed the tracks, being careful when approaching any high ground. Then Jim noticed dust in the distance. He motioned to Jack, who looked up. They dismounted just below a rise and walked slowly to the top, getting down on all fours to crawl the last few feet. Peeking over the top of the ridge, they saw a long line of riders. And the riders were carrying lances. You couldn't tell from that distance if the horses had feathers braided in their mane or not nor could you tell if they were wearing war paint. But it was still obvious it was a party of warriors.

"It's a war party," Jack said. "They don't make a line like that when they are hunting. We'd better get back to camp and get ready." So they made it back down the ridge, mounted, and headed back to their box canyon. If they saw the dust of the Indian ponies, you can be sure that the Indians would have seen their dust too.

When they reached their camp, they immediately started beefing up their fortifications. They started getting out spare ammunition from their saddlebags and packs. Jim had an 1866 Henry .44 caliber carbine. He noticed that Jack had a .44 Henry rifle also. Joe and Sam both had Spencer .56 carbines they had scrounged from the battlefield during the war. They held seven shots each with the magazine inside the butt stock. Jim's carbine held twelve shots, and Jack's Henry held eighteen. They each had a six-gun. Jim had a Colt .45 Army revolver that shot loose ammunition, but he had a spare cylinder for it. And he had a spare Colt he normally kept in his saddlebags. He dug it out and reloaded it as well as the spare cylinders. The six-gun in his holster was already loaded.

So everyone made preparations for a battle with the Indians in case it came. And it would probably come.

Jim and Joe pushed the horse herd to the back end of the box canyon. Jack had found a place near camp behind a rock to stand guard where he'd have good cover but could also watch the entrance to the canyon. It had a narrow entrance, with the sides of the canyon going up steeply. So it looked to him like the only way they could get into the canyon was through the entrance.

Sam fell to, cooking them some supper. They'd have to eat.

Jack said, "They will probably attack at dawn. That is an Apache's favorite time to attack. They'll steal horses during the night if they think they can do so without a fight. But they don't like to fight at night. Superstitious."

Of course, Jim already knew that. But neither Joe nor Sam had fought Indians before. They were learning lots of new things.

They came in one at a time to eat supper. Then they kept one man guarding the herd and another watching the opening. They would maintain this watch all night. Only two could sleep at a time. They really needed more men, Jim decided. Jack was thinking the same. But they were stuck with their crew of four for now. And Jim remembered Jack saying that four men was the minimum. They were definitely the minimum number they could get by with.

The Indians did attack at dawn. Jack was at his lookout post and watched them seem to just come up out of the ground. He shot the first one he saw and then downed two more braves that were running toward them, holding their lances at the ready. One of them threw his lance just before he was shot. It missed Jack's head by about two inches.

Sam ran to his spot at the rock just to the west of the camp, and he opened fire as well. Jim and Joe were still down at the far end of the canyon, keeping the horses close herded. When they heard the gunfire, they headed their horses to where the fighting was going on, running them in a zigzag pattern to make it hard for an Apache arrow to connect. And several were fired at them. When they were in range, they dismounted so they could hug the ground and started shooting. Jim worked the lever on his rifle as fast as he could and kept firing everywhere he thought an Indian would be.

The attack only lasted a few minutes. The Apaches had quickly learned that they didn't have the element of surprise and broke off. But Jim knew they would lay siege to them. There was water from a creek flowing through the canyon so the horses had water. And they had filled all their canteens the day before. They could only settle down to watch and wait for now. Jim and Joe went back to the horse herd. They found their horses had run back and rejoined the herd when they dismounted to join the battle. Jim managed to catch his horse. He mounted him and rode over to catch Joe's horse. They rode them to a small tree in a low place behind the rocks where their defenses were and tied them there.

It was midmorning when the Apaches tried another attack. They might have thought they had relaxed their vigil by now. But all four riflemen were ready and shot them down as soon as they showed themselves. Four more dead Apaches, then nothing. Jim saw a tumbleweed blowing toward their position. He immediately fired into it. He heard the splat of his bullet striking flesh. The tumbleweed moved on with the wind, but a dead warrior lay on the ground behind it.

Then the Indians were gone again. They were just waiting and watching. The waiting was harder than fighting, Jim thought, and having to be on constant watch and continuously alert. The horse herd was still at the far end of the canyon, so they didn't need riders herding them. They seemed contented to stay where they were and just graze.

In the middle of the afternoon, it got hot. It was January, but it still got hot. There was still no sign of Indians.

"If they lose enough warriors, they'll quit," Jack told them. "They want our horses, and they want scalps. But if the cost in warriors killed is too great, they'll give up and leave."

"But do you think they're still out there?" Jim asked him.

"Yes, they're still out there. We've killed over half a dozen of them and possibly wounded several more. So that's heavy losses, but they haven't given up yet."

"How can you tell?" Jim decided to ask.

"No birds singing or frogs croaking," Jack answered. "There are birds in the trees along the creek, and there will also be frogs. But if there is danger nearby, they can sense it and will remain silent."

When evening approached, Jack decided to take some brush and make a bonfire where it would keep the approach to the canyon lit up during the night. The other three men kept him covered when he went out and started the fire. He built the fire close enough so that they could toss logs on it from the rock at the west side of their camp. They'd keep it going all night.

They kept two men on guard watching the entrance to the canyon all night long. Jack and Sam took the first watch. After four hours, they woke Jim and Joe, who took the next watch. Nothing happened during the night.

The Apaches attacked again at dawn the next morning. All four men were ready and shot a half dozen more braves. They couldn't have had more than a couple of dozen braves in their war party. They'd killed over half of them by now. But they continued to watch the opening of the canyon vigilantly all day. They looked toward their horse herd occasionally to make sure they were still there.

It was on the third morning that they woke up to birds singing and frogs croaking. So they knew the Indians had left.

Jim felt tired. He knew the other men were tired too. But all four men fell to, getting the fire going, making coffee, and cooking breakfast.

And when they left camp, they rode around in a circle looking for Indian sign. The only fresh tracks they found were those of unshod ponies heading back to the northwest.

CHAPTER 12

Herd Breaking

"What I think we should do now is finish herd breaking the horses we've got. Then find a buyer for the mares," Jack said at the campfire that night.

"And that will give the geldings time to heal up from being branded and gelded," Jim remarked.

"Yep," Jack answered.

"Do both of you agree?" Jack looked first toward Joe, then Sam.

"You're the one that knows mustanging," Joe then said. "That sounds like a good plan to me."

They had forty-two mares, most of which should foal in the spring. And they had thirty-eight weaned colts. They decided to keep the thirty-four geldings and saddle break them when they got a chance. Jack had brought forty-four horses in all. Jim had his two, Joe one, and Sam three. So they had fifty tame horses. They had their four saddle horses and two packhorses to carry their supplies. That left forty-four tame horses that could each be roped to a mustang. With their stallion dead, they figured it wouldn't take as long to herd break the mares. And the colts would, of course, be accustomed to running with the grown stock in the herd they were born in.

The next morning, after breakfast, they went out to the herd, and Jack shook out a loop. He roped a mouse-colored gelding's front feet so he could throw him. Jim was ready with a piggin' string and tied his feet. Joe had roped one of the tame horses, a bay with a white spot on his nose. They tied one end of the rope around the mouse-colored gelding's neck and the other around the neck of the tame horse. Then Jim untied the pony's feet so he could get up.

Then the mustang took off to run but, of course, dragged the bay with him. The bay ran along behind him to keep from being dragged down, but after fighting the rope a few minutes, the mustang settled down.

They repeated the process with all the mustangs. They ran out of tame horses before they got to all the weaned colts, so they just left them with one front foot tied to a back foot. Then they broke camp and got them moving east. The sunshine was bright, and Joe and Sam rode drag the first part of the day. They pulled their bandanas up over their noses to keep from breathing the dust. They made their noon camp and cooked and ate as quickly as they could while the horses were grazing. Then they loaded up the packhorses and started out again.

They found a place near a creek to camp for the night. Joe and Sam took the first night guard. They had 130 head of horses in all, counting their saddle horses. Jack and Jim kept a night horse saddled and tied. They were back into country, where there were occasional mesquite bushes. When it came time to relieve the other two guards, they rolled out of their blankets, stamped their boots on, and mounted up.

After a breakfast of bacon and biscuits and gravy and coffee, they saddled fresh mounts, bunched up the horse herd, and headed them east again. They had passed a ranchero owned by a Mexican rancher on their way to their mustang hunting grounds. That was where they were headed now to see if he wanted to buy some broodmares.

They kept on seeing wild cattle as they continued to drive the horses east. They expected the ranchero to be about a week's ride from their mustanging grounds.

Jack and Jim rode point, and Joe and Sam took the flank positions this time, moving back to the drag position when needed to haze any stragglers along. They had been on the trail for three days when half a dozen riders appeared ahead of them. Jack and Jim had started riding with their rifles across their saddles. When the horse herd saw riders in their path, they pulled up, as did both Jim and Jack with their rifles pointing across the pommels of their saddles but held in both hands. Jim felt pretty sure the one he saw in the middle was the leader of the group. So he figured he'd shoot him first if they drew guns and started shooting. Joe and Sam saw what was happening and hurried up to join Jim and Jack on each side.

It was six against four, but none of the strange riders had drawn a gun yet.

"Howdy, strangers, state your business," Jack spoke first.

"We're looking for a herd of stolen horses," the leader said.

"Well, this ain't them. Every one of them is branded either with the Rolling JW brand or the 4 Bar C," Jack replied. "I own the Rolling JW spread just a week's ride or so to the east of here. We've been mustanging and have some wild stock in the herd. We branded them with the 4 Bar C brand, which is our trail brand."

"We're gonna cut the herd," came the reply from the leader.

"You won't cut the herd," Jack answered. "You can ride by and look at brands if you wish, but you won't move a single horse out of the herd."

"Okay. Just so they aren't stolen horses," he said in reply. They saw the rifles Jack and Jim were both holding.

So three of the men went to one side and the other three to the other. They allowed them to move their herd on past them, moving them slow enough so they could see the brands. They had branded the mares on the neck because they figured whoever bought them would want to slap a brand on their hip.

The men couldn't find anything that looked like stolen stock, so they let them go on by. After another couple of days, they drew near to the ranchero. Just before noon, they pulled up and made their noon camp. Jack knew it would be time for their siesta. So they waited until about four o'clock by the sun, then Jack rode down to the ranch buildings to see if he could find the Don at home. He returned in about thirty minutes or so with the Don and two vaqueros to look at the mares. The Don was an elderly man with gray hair and riding a blue roan.

"Hello. I'm Don Luis Diego," he said. There was only a trace of a Spanish accent to his voice.

"I'm Jack, and this is Jim, Joe, and Sam," Jack told him. He gestured toward each man when introducing them.

Jim had Joe and Sam help him cut the mares and weaned colts out of the herd and put them in a separate herd. Don Luis looked them over, then said to Jack, "You and your crew are invited to dinner at my ranchero tonight. You can run your horses into a small pasture near the corral so you won't have to watch them."

This caught all four men by surprise. They weren't aware of the hospitality you'd sometimes receive from a Mexican rancher if he liked you. And they had apparently made a good impression on him.

They drove the horses to the ranchero's headquarters and ran them into the corral. They dismounted, unsaddled their mounts, and put their saddles and bridles on the top corral panel. They followed the Don and his two vaqueros to the cookshack.

They walked in, and the Don introduced them to all the vaqueros. He said something in Spanish to the men. "He told them we have guests for dinner tonight," Jose told them. Since they were guests, they went through the serving line first. The cook placed a burrito with chili sauce, some refried beans, and fried rice on their plates. And he had a big pot of coffee, so they filled up a cup each.

After they took their grub to one of the tables, the vaqueros went through the line and got their plates and coffee cups filled. Joe took a fork and knife and cut off a piece of the burrito and sampled it. It tasted delicious. It was made of beef that had apparently been boiled and shredded. It was his first time to have Mexican food. He was accustomed to the Southern food that he had grown up with. He had found that the food served in Texas wasn't much different from what was common in South Carolina, except on a Texas ranch, you had beef every day and never had chicken or pork—except for bacon, which was very popular at breakfast time.

"So how are things on the frontier?" Don Luis asked.

"Plenty wild," Jim answered.

"Have any trouble with Indians?"

"Yes, we did have a fight with the Apaches," Jim answered. "They apparently were planning to steal our horses."

The Don just looked at him expectantly as if he were waiting for him to finish a sentence.

"The fight lasted three days. They didn't get any of our horses."

It appeared that the Don enjoyed their company. He apparently liked having guests for dinner occasionally. But these were also men that could fight if they had a three-day fight with Apaches and still not lose any of their horses.

After they had eaten, he told them they could unroll their bedrolls out near the corral. That's what the vaqueros frequently did in the summers when it was hot.

So it was morning before Don Luis looked at the horses they had for sale. He agreed to buy all the mares and colts. After some brief bickering, he bought the mares for five dollars a head and the colts for two dollars. He paid for them in cash, and Jim made out a bill of sale. All four mustangers signed it.

So they netted $286 for their first sale of mustangs. They moved the herd on farther east to a likely place to make camp for the night. They were far enough away from the mustang's home grounds that they were able to remove all the ropes yoking them to tame stock. And they removed the hobbles from the colts. They were pretty well herd broke by now, and the geldings had healed. They could start saddle breaking the geldings whenever they were ready.

They made camp that night, and after supper, Jim and Joe got out their mouth organs again and serenaded the coyotes. They felt like they had something to celebrate. They had survived a fight with Apaches and managed a catch of a decent herd of mustangs. And they felt like they did pretty good for their first gather.

C H A P T E R   1 3

Bronc Busting

They decided to take the wild geldings to Jack's ranch to saddle break them there. Jack explained it would take about a month to get them accustomed enough to the saddle to be of any use. So they took the rest of their horses on east. It was about another week's ride to Jack's place.

When they arrived, they noticed smoke coming from the chimney of the cabin. Jack rode up, and his pa came out.

"Howdy, son. I just came out to check on your place. You'd been gone long enough that I wanted to make sure no squatters had come out and taken over."

"I appreciate it, Pa," Jack said. "We got a pretty good catch of mustangs. Wanna see 'em?" The other three men were in the process of running them into the corral.

They cut out all the horses that they had started with and put them into a smaller adjoining corral. Jack went to the pump and started pumping water into the horse trough. He figured the first thing they would want was water. Then they turned all the tame horses out into the pasture except for four of them and, of course, Hal's horse. They wanted a horse for each of them for when they needed it. The wild ones to be broke to the saddle were left in the main corral. Then they unsaddled the four horses and went to the cabin to cook supper. Hal already had some coffee made. They had plenty of firewood left over from when they had been at the ranch before. So they built a fire out in front of the cabin and cooked up some beef and beans and biscuits and gravy and coffee. After they'd eaten, they rolled a smoke each and sat around the campfire puffing their cigarettes. It was dark by then. And they were tired. They had a right to be. Jim, Joe, and Sam unrolled their sleeping bags and slept outside as before, letting Jack and Hal have the two bunks in the cabin. Jim and Jack preferred to sleep outside, but it seemed natural for Jack to sleep inside this time since his father was there. It was chilly, but there was no snow.

The next morning, Hal decided he'd better ride back to his own ranch. He was perfectly willing to leave the horse breaking to the young men.

They had thirty-four wild mustangs to saddle break. The next morning, they got up and got an early breakfast as usual. It was barely getting to be daylight when they went out to the corral. Jack decided he'd go first. Joe and Sam sat on the top rail of the corral to watch the show. Jack went out and roped what looked like a four-year-old dapple gray and put a hackamore on him and tied him to the snubbing post. He put a blindfold on him and then he saddled him. He untied the hackamore rope from the snubbing post and hopped up onto his back. He then reached down and undid the blindfold. He took off bucking. Jack rode really well. He just kept on riding and letting the horse buck until his sides started heaving. He finally slowed to a walk and then just stopped so he could catch his breath. He was covered with lather by then. Jack hadn't touched him with his spurs yet. He now spurred him forward and made him walk around the corral a little. Then he rode him over to the fence and dismounted.

"I'm next," Jim said. He already had his rope in his hand and shook out a loop. He roped a buckskin and repeated the process that Jack had just done. He kept his seat and rode his bronc to a walk with no problem too.

Joe wanted a piece of the action by then. His roping still needed work. He had to try three times before he finally managed to get his loop on a bronc. He made use of the snubbing post at one end of the corral and blindfolded his bronc just like he had seen Jack and Jim do. He saddled him and put a hackamore on him. Then he climbed on. He hadn't been riding all day every day all summer the previous

61

summer as had Jack and Jim. But the riding he'd done in the past couple of months had helped get him in shape. He succeeded in riding him to a walk, but you could tell that Joe was in worse shape than the bronc after he finished his ride.

They had thirty-one more mustangs to go. "Every horse in the bunch needs to be rode to a walk once a day every day for a month in order to be considered rough broke," Jack said. He looked toward Sam and asked, "Do you want a go at it?"

"Yep," answered Sam. He repeated the steps that Joe had done using the snubbing post. He climbed on and released the blindfold. He lasted three bucks and got thrown. He jumped up unhurt while Jack roped the bronc's front legs, throwing him, and tied his legs. He blindfolded him again. Sam got on him again, determined to complete his ride. Jack removed the blindfold and untied his legs. He got up and started bucking again. Sam lasted him out this time.

The next time, it came Jack's turn, and he got his rope on a black gelding, Jim knew he had trouble as soon as he saw the rope snag the mustang's front feet. When the gelding hit the ground, Jack ran up to the back of the bronc, leaned over, and tied his feet and had to dodge his snapping teeth three times before getting him tied. He couldn't get the saddle in place due to having to dodge those sharp teeth. Jim got his rope and put it around the horse's neck, pulling it tight and holding his head forward, and Jack put the blindfold on him. Jack then managed to finish saddling him.

Jack put the hackamore on his head before removing the rope from his neck. Jack got in position in the saddle and then reached down and released the horse's feet then untied the blindfold. The black got up fighting and snorting, and Jim could tell by the fire in his eyes that he was made out of pure hate. And Jim hadn't seen bucking any fiercer than that before. Jack did a good job of staying on him until the black bucked three times very vigorously and then changed directions. Jack lost his seat then. The bronc immediately went for Jack and would have killed him. He ran up and would have stomped Jack to death with his front feet, but Jack rolled out of the way. His jaws were open and ready to grab a mouthful of Jack's shoulder. But a shot rang out, and the black dropped. Everyone turned to look at Jim, who was holding a smoking Colt.

"Hey, you killed my horse!" Jack complained.

"I know. He would have killed you," Jim returned.

"How can I break a horse to ride when you keep shooting them?" Jack had a note of humor in his voice. He knew Jim had saved his life.

They decided it was time to stop for chuck, so Jack coiled up his rope. Jack removed the saddle and hackamore from the black, and Joe and Sam each put a rope on him and dragged him out of the corral. Jim opened the gate for them, and Jack kept the other broncs bunched in the far end of the corral while they drug the carcass out. They dragged the dead horse down to a gully, rolled it in, and then caved in dirt enough to cover it.

After chuck, they went back to the corral to resume their day's work. They now started doing two mustangs at a time. Jim got astride one and Jack another. After riding their broncs to a walk, they unsaddled and turned them loose. Then after that, they let Joe and Sam have another go.

When they knocked off for the night, Jack started pumping the horse trough full of water, and Jim climbed up into the loft of the barn and forked down enough hay for the hungry horses. Then they were up at sunrise again the next morning to start again. They'd managed to get a saddle on about half of them by noon every day. Joe or Sam one would usually knock off at about eleven o'clock or so by the sun to cook dinner. Joe and Sam took turns with the cooking. Then everyone came back after dinner and rode the rest of the broncs. They made sure that each bronc got ridden at least once every day.

After about a week, at the end of the day, they went to the fire and had chuck. Sam had done the cooking that night. When they finished eating, Jack mentioned they were nearly out of beef again.

"Would you and Sam be willing to ride out first thing in the morning and go find a recently weaned steer calf and rope him and bring him back to the cabin? Then shoot and butcher him? You can get in on more of the horse breaking when you're done quartering the meat."

So that morning, Jack and Jim went back out to the corral to resume their bronc busting, and Joe and Sam rode out looking for a weaning-sized calf. They were secretly glad to get a break from the bronc busting.

*****

After about three weeks, while sitting at the fire in the evening, Jack suggested to the other three men, "I think maybe we should consider wild cow hunting next instead of going after more broncs. We haven't made that much money mustanging yet. But with the railroad in Kansas now, we could put together a pretty good-sized herd of longhorns, trail break them, brand them, and take them north to Abilene. Before the winter is over, we could probably have several thousand head of longhorns trail broke and ready to brand." The other three mustangers agreed.

CHAPTER 14

Wild Cow Hunting

"We'll need a chuck wagon and more hands," Jim mused when they saddled up that morning. The freshly broke broncs had been added to their cavvy, and that would help since they needed the extra horses, especially after hiring more riders.

Jack nodded and said, "We can use my horse herd again. We'll need about eighty or ninety horses in all. My forty head plus the thirty-three we just finished saddle breaking and the eight personal horses we originally started with makes eighty-two. And I want my share of the green broke broncs to get rode regularly. I think we have enough horses."

"We can buy a chuck wagon with the money we got for selling the herd of mares and should still have some left to pay wages with," Jim added.

"I'll stay behind and loose herd the horses if you like," Sam volunteered.

"Yeah, we want to make sure the new broncs have accepted their new home," Jack said.

The other three men saddled up and headed for the small town of Killeen to look for a chuck wagon. And they stopped at each farm they came to and checked to see if there was a teenage boy wanting a job as a cowhand. Jack figured they would need about fifteen men.

Along the way, they managed to find eight farm boys wanting work. There wasn't much farming going on in the wintertime anyway. It was February by now. Killeen wasn't much of a town. It had a general store, a courthouse, a church, and five saloons. But it also had a hostler and a horse trader that sold wagons. When they reached town, they rode to the wagon yard where wagons were for sale.

Jim picked out the wagon he wanted and, after some brief bickering, bought it. "Do you have any work horses?" Jim asked the trader.

"Sure do," answered the trader and led them to a nearby corral.

"There's a pair that is used to pulling together," the trader pointed to two bay horses.

"We want young horses!" said Jim vehemently.

The trader was just getting geared for his sales pitch and intended to claim they were young but didn't. Jim picked out a horse he thought was built right and walked up, grabbed its lower jaw, and checked its mouth.

"About seven years old," he said. "What do you want for this one?"

"Forty dollars," said the trader.

"We'll ride over to the next town and see what we can find" was Jim's answer to that.

The trader started his sales pitch, but Jack and Jim both started walking off.

"I'll take thirty dollars for him."

"You'll take twenty dollars or forget it" was Jim's answer.

"You need a team. I'll take fifty dollars for him and his mate." The horse standing next to him looked like a good wagon horse. Jim checked his mouth and decided he was about ten years old.

So they bought the two horses for forty dollars. They now had a good used chuck wagon and a team of horses to pull it.

"I want another team so we'll have a spare," Jim then said.

So they repeated the process in a similar fashion. Jack mainly just looked on silently while Jim made the trade. It appeared that Jim knew horse trading.

They hired a cook. They went over to the saloon to see if there were any cowboys looking for work. They managed to hire six more men that way—experienced cowhands. They figured that was enough to start with. They could hire more men later.

So with the cook driving the chuck wagon and one of greenies (named Billy) wrangling the horse cavvy, fifteen cowboys started out for the wild cow hunting grounds. It would be at least two weeks before they could get out beyond any settled land into Indian country, where all cattle were mavericks.

"Another advantage to hunting wild cattle," Jack explained to them, "is that the Indians normally don't take it personal when you round up cattle and drive them off. The Indians are especially fond of horse flesh. And they like buffalo meat. And pulling cattle off the range just increased the carrying capacity of the range for mustangs and buffalo. Not that Indians look ahead that much. They still might attack if they're looking for scalps, or they might try to steal our horse cavvy just on general principle. But we'll draw more attention from Indians rounding up wild horses than we will with wild cattle."

They started running low on meat again since they were feeding a much bigger crew. Jack and Jim tended to scout ahead as much as they could to make sure there were no surprises ahead of them. They decided they'd be on the lookout for meat if they saw anything to shoot. Jim saw a herd of antelope and shot one and brought it back behind his saddle. It was to hopefully last them another week or two.

Jim had never tasted antelope meat before. He found out very quickly at the fire that night that he liked beef or buffalo meat much better than he did antelope meat. They just had a better flavor. But meat was meat, and he didn't complain.

Three days later, Jack came back with the carcass of a buffalo calf tied behind his saddle. And Jim was glad to have the improvement added to their diet. The cook had loaded up on whatever supplies he needed before they left town. So they had buffalo meat and spuds, beans, biscuits, and gravy. Sometimes, Cookie made cornbread instead of biscuits for variety. And he had bought some dried apples when he stocked up on supplies and baked them a few apple pies a couple of times a week. They still ate antelope meat once every two or three days—didn't want to waste it. But they ate buffalo meat more often. Their crew was starting to shape up like a regular cow outfit.

After a couple of weeks of traveling, they started seeing more and more wild cattle. They spooked and stampeded as soon as they saw them.

They reached a point that was near a creek that looked like a decent campsite. "I think we should make a semipermanent camp here and start our gather," said Jack.

"Yep," said Jim. Joe and Sam just nodded.

That night at the campfire, Jack said, "We're far enough west of the frontier that I think we'd better double the guard on the horses tonight."

"I think so too," said Jim.

Each man kept a night horse tied either to a tree or a stake driven in the ground when they rolled up in their blankets to go to sleep that night.

Jim had his night guard scheduled for 2:00 a.m. When one of the new hands, Zeke, came to wake him up, he looked up at the position of the Big Dipper. It showed that it was about two in the morning. There was no moon, but the stars were out. He mounted his night horse and rode out to the horse herd. He saw Joe riding out too. They were relieving Zeke and Bill. They had more cowboys this time, so they didn't have to stand guard as often now. When Bill saw them, he turned his horse to ride back to camp. The stars were really bright this night, but there was no moon. And there was a light breeze. There was nothing stirring other than that.

Jim started riding around the herd going one way, and Joe went the other. They just rode slowly around the horse herd and met at the opposite end. Then they turned around to ride back. You could barely see the horses in the cavvy in the starlight. They appeared to be sleeping. Most of them slept standing up, though, in some cases, a horse will lie down to sleep.

Jim looked all around, looking for any sign of movement in the darkness and listening for any sounds as well. All was quiet this time of night. It was so cool and peaceful. At the opposite end of the horse herd, he saw Joe moving toward him from the other side. He halted his horse, waved, and started riding back the other direction.

It had been Jim's idea for he and Joe to take their night guard in the wee hours of the morning. He and Jack were the most experienced Indian fighters in the crew—except for maybe the six experienced cowboys they had hired. But they hadn't had time to get to know them yet. They were unknown quantities at this time.

When it was 4:00 a.m. by the Big Dipper, Jim rode back to camp to wake his relief, and he heard a war hoop and the sound of running hooves. He didn't dismount but just wheeled his horse and started him running back to the herd. The men asleep were awake instantly. They tightened their cinches and mounted up, heading toward the stampeding horses.

You could barely see the ground in the starlight. But once Jim got his horses headed toward the disappearing horse herd, he just gave him his head. He knew a horse could see better at night than a man could.

Jim was riding his buckskin. He had turned out to be the best night horse in his string. And Buck seemed to know what to do. He ran all out to catch the stampeding horses. Jim reached down to his saddle boot and pulled his rifle out. When he saw a paint horse ahead of him, he simply raised his rifle up and fired. He saw a blur of something hitting the ground, so he apparently managed to hit the Indian. It was a lucky shot because he was running at a full gallop. He worked the lever on his Henry and saw another Indian pony. He saw no rider this time, but he knew about the practice of Indians riding on the far side of their horses to avoid being seen. He simply shot the horse.

As Jim worked the lever of his rifle again, he thought about how it was convenient that the Indians all preferred paint horses. The cowboys always rode solid-colored horses. That way, you could always tell the difference even at nighttime when you barely had any light at all.

Jim felt the whiz of a bullet just missing his brisket by inches. So these Indians had rifles! He turned his rifle toward where the bullet seemed to come from and looked for anything moving. He saw a bit of white on brown and leveled his rifle and fired. The pinto made a half somersault. Jim levered in a new shell into his rifle and halted

69

and wheeled his horse. He saw the flash of the Indian's rifle as he fired again and fired at the flash. The flash was near the ground, so Jim concluded the shot came from the dismounted Indian. He couldn't hear the bullet hit due to the sound of the horses' hooves, so he didn't know if he'd hit him or not. He worked his reins back and forth to keep the buckskin moving in a zigzag pattern and felt another bullet whiz by his head. He reined his horse to a halt and immediately brought his rifle up and fired at the flash. Then he levered in another shell and pulled his rifle up again. He saw another flash and fired directly at it. This time, there was no return fire, so he must have got him. He spurred his horse back into a run to pursue the stampeding cavvy again.

Jim estimated they had to run with the stampeding horses for probably half an hour, but they finally started to slow down. The Indians must have been outnumbered because by the time they had the horse cavvy turned and started them to milling, the Indians were all gone.

They headed the horse cavvy back toward their camp. They were in Comanche country. They had expected attempts to steal their horses and were ready for them this time. But they hadn't expected the Indians to be armed with rifles! Someone must be trading guns to the Indians!

CHAPTER 15

Mean Mavericks

They started to explore their hunting grounds. They saw wild cattle ever so often. So they halted for the night and decided they'd start gathering cattle first thing in the morning. Over the campfire that night, Jack had all the cowboys gather around, and he briefed them on what to do.

"When we ride out in the morning, we'll need to spread out in a V-shaped formation and start moving northward across the plains. When we see cattle, they'll stampede. We'll follow them, keeping our horses at an easy lope. If the cattle go over a rise and you think you've lost them, you'll see them again in a few minutes. When you do, they'll stampede all over again. Any new bunches of cattle you see will stampede too. Try to haze them over into one herd.

"The biggest hazard to running wild cattle is that the bulls are vicious and may charge your horse. He'll gore and kill the horse if he can. The cows are plenty vicious too, but the bulls are the worst. You can shoot their horns near their head and it will stun them and sometimes take the fight out of them. But if you have to shoot them to save yourself or your horse, just shoot them between the eyes. That is perfectly okay to do. We want you alive and we want your horse alive.

"After a few hours, the wild cattle will slow to a steady trot. Then you'll have to keep them running continuously day and night for at least two days. Billy, you will be in charge of horse wrangling.

You'll bring the horse cavvy up so that the cowboys can change horses every three or four hours."

This meant that the cattle would have to go two days without food or sleep but also that the cowboys would have to do the same. At the end of the two days, they should get the cattle shaped into a milling herd.

So the next morning after breakfast, they saddled up and started out. They had put together a rope corral to run the cavvy into. After each man saddled up and left, the horse wrangler let the horses out. He'd let them graze and then run them up so they'd be near the riders after three hours or so. They made their V-shaped line and got started. It was barely daylight when they saw their first bunch of wild cattle. They took off running immediately as soon as they saw them. The cowboys just kept their horses in an easy lope and followed them per Jack's instructions. After fifteen minutes or so, another bunch looked up and saw them coming and took off running as well. In a few hours, they had what looked like several hundred head of stock rushing toward the horizon, fogging up dust a hundred feet high.

Their horses ran into a lather, white foam covering the horse from head to tail. At about midmorning, the wrangler brought up the cavvy so that each cowboy could drop back and rope a horse and change saddles.

Jim rode up to the cavvy and picked out the horse he wanted. He roped him and then rode away from the cavvy so he wouldn't interfere with the other cowboys changing horses. He pulled his horse to a stop and pulled in his rope. He unsaddled his horse, pulled the blanket off, and laid the saddle and blanket on the ground. Then he reached up and removed his bridle. Then he pulled in his fresh horse, put the bridle on him, and then threw on the saddle blanket. When he had it in place, he put on the saddle. He had to throw it on with one hand because he had to hold the horse's head with his left. He had to pull the cinch through the cinch ring with his horse dancing around. It required several rounds through the cinch ring. Then he cinched it tight. He pulled it through the top slit and wrapped it around twice and pulled it through the slit again. Then he removed the rope from his neck, gathered up the reins, and threw one under his neck. He grabbed both reins, mounted, and started coiling up his rope. He had a hook to the right of his saddle horn to lay his rope into. The spent horses that were turned loose lay down to roll and follow the cavvy at their leisure after getting their wind back.

Shortly after noon, it was time for the cowboys to change horses again. The herd had grown up to maybe seven hundred or eight hundred in size by then. They kept them going in a steady trot. When they tried to slow down or stop, the cowboys fired their guns in the air to spook them and get them going again. The longhorns had never heard a gunshot before. And they'd never seen a white man before. They'd seen Indians on occasion.

Jim hadn't noticed being tired especially due to the excitement. But he did get hungry after the sun went past the point of being directly overhead. He knew there would be no time to eat.

Then one of the bulls decided to charge Jim's horse. He saw the hate in his eyes as he started his lunge. Jack saw him too and swung his rope. Jim had his rope out and was ready. Jack had turned his horse around with his back to the bull so that when he hit the end of the rope, he turned a half somersault. He hit the ground but got up snorting and fighting and headed for Jack's horse. Then Jim swung his rope. Jim turned his horse around with his back to the bull the same way Jack had done. So when he hit the end of Jim's rope, he turned to attack Jim again, but Jack's rope held fast.

The bull really did go crazy then. Caught between two ropes, he couldn't attack either of the two men that he hated. He snorted and bucked and fumed, but the two ropes held tight.

They just maneuvered their horses to keep him between them. It was probably ten or fifteen minutes before he finally found out he was only giving himself a beating, so he headed back to the herd. The two cowboys rode up beside him to loosen their ropes so they could shake them loose from his horns. Then they rode away from the stampeding longhorns long enough to coil their ropes up to have them ready the next time they needed them.

One bull was especially vicious. He refused to stampede with the rest of the herd but charged the first horse he came to. No one had time to rope him. He charged the horse of one of the greenies.

The greenie tried to maneuver his horse clear, but the bull managed to gore the horse in the flank. The horse went down, of course, and the bull went for the rider. He tried to yank out his six-shooter, but the thong was still in place. So he jumped to the side, barely missing the sharp horns of the bull. The bull turned to charge him again, but that gave Jim and Jack time to get in position to rope the bull. After making him turn a half somersault three times, Jim finally dismounted and managed to get him hog-tied. They took time out to make him into a steer before letting him up. He was considerably subdued when he finally rose to his feet again.

Jim had to put the poor horse out of his misery. He was still on the ground with his belly laid open, blood everywhere, but still thrashing his feet and squealing. Jim shot him in the head. He hated shooting a good horse, but he hated seeing him suffer even worse. There was no way a horse could recover from a wound that severe.

Jim had the greenie get up on his horse behind him and took him to the cavvy to get another horse. Jack rode with them with the greenie's saddle and bridle tied to the back of his horse.

The greenie was named Dale. Jim let him off at the horse cavvy, and Jack dismounted to untie and unload his saddle and bridle. He had tied it pommel up behind his own saddle. Dale's rope was tied to his saddle, so he untied it so he could rope a fresh horse.

They went back to the running cattle, and this time, a cow charged Jim's horse. They were mean too, just like the bulls but not as strong. Jim pulled his gun and shot the tip of her horn off. She turned a half somersault and fell. Stunned, Jim just left her lying there. He knew she'd come to in a few minutes and get up.

The men were exhausted by nightfall. And they were even hungrier. But the horse wranglers brought up the horse herd and each one in turn roped a fresh mount, changed his saddle, remounted, and resumed the chase.

By midnight, Jim was so tired that he ached all over. They hadn't had time to eat since morning, so he was ravenously hungry. He was still sitting his saddle when morning came, and he was numb. They changed horses every three hours or so, but the cowboys were expected to keep going without letup. The size of the herd had grown to about two thousand or so.

By the end of the second day, they probably had over twenty-five hundred head of longhorns. But they continued the chase on into the night. All night long, they plodded and yelled and fired their guns if the cattle tried to stop. Finally, at dawn the next day, they got the cattle to milling into one big massive herd. They were soaked with sweat as were the cowboys and their horses.

The chuck wagon caught up with them, and the cook started fixing chuck for the starving, exhausted cowboys. As soon as they had fed, half of them were allowed to go to their bedrolls and grab some sleep. The other half had to stick with the herd and keep them bunched up. After about six hours or so of sleep, the rested cowboys got up, had chuck again, and then saddled up to relieve the men guarding the herd.

It took another two days to get the men and horses recuperated enough to string the cattle out and get them moving as a herd. Jim and Jack took a tally to see how many they finally wound up with. Jim counted 3,438, and Jack counted 3,442. So they figured they had a pretty good herd. They strung them out and headed them toward Jack's ranch. They'd brand them with their trail brand and get ready to start their drive north.

It took about three weeks to get the herd to Jack's spread. They had managed to water in a river just before they arrived on the Rolling JW Ranch. Jack thought that was good. This way, they'd be waterlogged and easier to handle while getting them settled down and located.

Jack and Jim rode into the county seat to register the 4 bar C brand while the cattle and horses were resting up from their ordeal.

CHAPTER 16

Horseshoeing and Branding

Jack had a blacksmith forge and an anvil in a toolshed near the barn. He also had some iron bars to make shoes for the newly broke horses. While they were looking at the horses in the corral, Jack said, "I think we should take time out to shoe the horses while we can."

None of the men had any experience shoeing horses except Jack. They needed a man to rope each horse and bring him to the blacksmith shop, which Joe and Sam did in turns.

Jim helped Jack make the horseshoes. The forge had a handle to turn to keep the air blowing onto the fire. Jim turned the handle on the forge while Jack took his tongs and gripped the bar of iron and held it to the fire until it was red hot. Then he held it there another few minutes until it turned blue. Then he moved it to the anvil and hammered it into the shape of a horseshoe. Then he heated the new shoe on the fire again. He then punched holes for the horseshoe nails. He had to have Jim hold the tongs gripping the horseshoe while he took a hammer and punch to make the nail holes.

When Sam brought up a horse, Jim put a hackamore on him and held his head, but Jack still had to dodge the hooves until he gripped one of them and lifted it. The horse stopped kicking while he was standing on just three feet. He trimmed the hoof first and then nailed the horseshoe in place. It was harder for the horse to kick when standing on just three feet, but Jim had to be alert to any attempts of the mustang to bite and had to hold his head firmly. Then, when all four shoes were in place, Jim removed the hackamore and turned the horse loose. Joe roped another bronc and brought it up to them so they could repeat the process. When they finished shoeing that mustang, Sam had already roped another bronc and had it ready for them.

It took four days to finish shoeing all the rough broke geldings. But they finally finished the job. After all the horses were shod, they added them to the horse cavvy. They'd get ridden frequently. Then it was time to start branding the cattle. They built a working chute out of logs to do the branding. They built it in a corner of the corral and set posts and used logs to build a chute leading into it. A branding chute would make the branding go a lot faster. They had to fell some trees to make posts and panels, but they built one wing going into the chute similar to how they rigged their horse trap earlier in the winter, except on a much smaller scale of course. The side of the corral served as the other wing. The working chute was built against the side of the corral nearest the pasture. There was a gate there where they could turn each steer loose after he was branded.

Then Jack went back to his forge and made some new branding irons. He had to have new irons for the 4-C brand. Jim manned the forge for him again while he heated each iron. They made four branding irons. Then Jack also made a couple of Slant JB irons since he knew Jim didn't have any.

"We'll run eight or ten head of cattle through the chute each hour this way," Jack said. "We wouldn't be able to do half that many if we had to rope and throw each critter."

They had sent the cowboys out each morning to round up any unbranded strays they could find and add them to the herd while they were engaged in their blacksmithing activities. They now sent the cowboys out to gather up about a hundred head of cattle and move them into the corral. After that, they crowded a bunch of them into the wings of the chute, forcing one cow critter into the chute at a time. They kept four branding irons going. Two of the greenies were assigned the task of keeping each brander supplied with a hot iron when he needed it. They also had the greenies working to keep the fire going by adding wood to it periodically. They had another greenie out chopping wood to keep the fuel supply ready.

Two greenies alternating brought branding irons from the fire, and Joe pulled down a lever that squeezed the critter good and tight while Jack slapped the brand on his left hip. If it was a bull, Jim stood ready with his hunting knife and went behind the critter and made him into a steer. He inserted a pole just behind the bull's hind legs and in front of the post on each side of the chute to keep him from kicking him. He kept a whet rock handy. He had to sharpen the knife periodically. He had to keep it really sharp.

They branded all the old cows and bulls with their trail brand. Some of the bulls had moss between their horns and down their backs.

There appeared to be about a thousand young cows in the herd. So Jack and Jim made a deal to split them and brand half of them with the Rolling JW and the other half with the Slant JB. Jack needed more mother cows for his spread, and Jim wanted to get a nest egg started for his ranch.

They picked out about forty young bulls that looked like good breeding stock and left them bulls when they branded them. Twenty of them were for Jack and another twenty were for Jim. The range was still open. They'd be okay to just turn loose for the summer. The cows would be dropping calves in a few months. So they'd have to round them up and brand their calves the following fall.

Lots of bawling and stomping and fighting went on as they ran cow after cow through the chute, with the branding iron sizzling as it made its mark on their thick hides. When a critter had been branded and released from the chute, they opened the gate to the pasture and let him out, and one of the cowboys hazed him over to a herd that four cowboys kept loose herded to keep them separate from the unbranded stock—except the young cows and bulls branded with Jack or Jim's brand, which were turned loose to range wherever they wished. They didn't add them to the main herd. They'd only have to cut them out later if they did. They continued to run a hundred head of unbranded stock into the corral at a time. It was just the same routine day after day. The smell of burnt hair and flesh became so customary they got used to it.

It took over a month to finish branding all the stock. Then it was time to get ready to make their drive north. Some of the greenies wanted to quit and draw their wages. Sam still had plenty of money left over from his winnings from playing poker the previous fall. So he forked out the money to pay the hands. Jack put it down in his tally book so Sam could be reimbursed when they sold the herd in Abilene. They had to find new hands to hire to take the place of the boys that quit.

So the last week of April, they bunched up a herd of 2,462 steers and old cows, stretched them out in a line, and got them started north. The chuck wagon had been stocked up and was rattling along to the side of the herd. Jim and Jack were riding point, and Sam and Joe were riding swing. They had managed to hire a few more experienced cowboys; so the new men weren't all greenies this time, but most of them still were. The ones they hired before they started their wild cow hunt that stuck with them were shaping up and wouldn't be classified as greenies much longer.

Heading North

Jim and Jack kept on riding point. They just continued to head north to the tune of cattle bawling. The bawling would settle down after an hour or so. When they reached the point that wasn't far from Waco, it was nearly noon. At the chuck wagon, Jim told Jack, Joe, and Sam he was going to ride into Waco and wouldn't return till the following morning. So after chuck, Joe took his position at the point while Jim rode on into Waco. He was looking really rangy since he hadn't had a shave in several months. He pulled up to the bathhouse first and went in and got a bath. He had put some spare clothes in his saddlebags before leaving the chuck wagon. When he came out of the bathhouse, he went next door to a barbershop and got a haircut and shave. Then he got on his buckskin gelding and rode over to the General Store.

When Vickie saw him, she squealed and ran around the counter like she always did and hit him at a full run. He had to grab her and swing her around twice to keep from being knocked down. Then she put her feet down and hugged him so tight he couldn't have pulled loose if he had tried. She turned her head up for a kiss. He met her kiss, and she still just held on and prolonged the kiss forever.

"I missed you," she said breathlessly. "And you were gone *so* long. And did you start a ranch yet?" she asked.

"Not yet," he answered.

"Did you catch some wild horses?" She knew that was what he had intended when he left.

"Yes, we caught a herd of wild horses, and then we went back to southwest Texas and caught a herd of wild cattle. We're on the way to Abilene now to sell them."

"You mean you're leaving again?" The disappointment showed on her face.

"The trip will take about six or seven weeks, I'd guess. But then it will take another few weeks to ride back. I'll be gone about a couple of months in all."

"When are you coming home to stay?" was her next question.

"I have three partners. I own a fourth of the herd. When I get back, I should have enough money to start a ranch. Then I want you to marry me."

She brightened up when he said that. She was seventeen now and was starting to think of herself as an old maid! She'd been waiting for her man for four long years—long, long years. But if their wedding day were getting closer, then she felt better.

Vickie's father walked up then and held out his hand. Vickie was still clinging to Jim, but he took his free hand and shook hands with Mr. Allen.

"So our prodigal son finally returns," he jived.

"Yep," answered Jim. "We caught a herd of wild cattle and are taking our herd to Kansas."

"I thought you had gone wild horse hunting," Mr. Allen said.

"We did. And we caught a couple of bunches of wild horses. We had to spend a month saddle breaking them. Then we decided to go after wild cattle. More money in them. And money is what's scarce around here these days. Money is what I need to get a ranch started.

Vickie told her father she wanted to leave work early, and he, of course, agreed. So she and Jim walked out. She lived only a few blocks from the store. Jim just led his horse so he could walk beside her. They walked around the back so he could unsaddle his horse and put him in Mr. Allen's stable. He left his chaps and spurs with his saddle.

When they went inside, Vickie's mother was surprised to see him, of course, and came to get her hug. "You were gone a long time," she said. "You know, you shouldn't leave my daughter alone so long. She's been pining for you."

"I've been pining for her too," he replied.

Vickie pulled him to the couch and told him to sit down. "Tell me what southwest Texas was like," she said.

"After you get past the brush country, it's mostly rolling prairie. You see bunches of wild cattle every little bit. And you'll also see herds of wild mustangs. They spook and run as soon as they see you. They're so wild."

He elaborated on how they had constructed a horse trap and pulled in a good bunch of horses after several tries. And then he went on to explain how they had caught a herd of mares. He didn't tell her about how Jack had to shoot that one stallion to avoid being killed by those powerful teeth. Or how he had shot the black gelding to keep Jack from being stomped to death. He didn't tell her about the Indian fight either.

Then he explained that when they took the mares to a ranch to sell them, they found out they weren't really going to make very much money mustanging. So they decided to round up some wild cattle. And he explained how in only a couple of days, they had what they'd need to make a big enough herd for a drive and how it took several weeks to brand them all and get them ready for the trip. And he also told her about the five hundred or so young cows he had branded with the Slant JB brand. "So we have the start of a herd now."

"But I thought you intended to start a horse ranch instead of a cattle ranch," she said.

"I do. But it takes too long to get a horse ranch going to the point that you can't make any money doing it. I decided I'd better raise horses *and* cattle starting out."

Mr. Allen came in from work. It was later than they realized. And Mrs. Allen had started supper. She came to the living room to greet Mr. Allen. Then she turned to Jim and Vickie and said, "I hope you plan to play music tonight. It's been ages since I've heard you play."

"Sounds good to me," Jim answered.

"Want to start tuning up now?" Vickie asked.

"Sure" was Jim's answer. So she ran to the other room to get Jim's mandolin. He always left it with her.

She came back and handed it to him and then sat down at her piano. He tuned the mandolin to her piano and then struck up a tune. He was a little rusty since he hadn't touched his mandolin since the previous fall. Naturally, the last time he played it would have been the last time he saw her. She started playing the background on her piano. Jim did several instrumentals to get warmed up, then he started singing. She joined in with the harmony. It sounded beautiful. And Vickie always got such a beautiful look on her face while she sang.

Louise came and called supper ready. So Jim set down his mandolin and got up. Vickie was on her feet by then. He took her hand and led her to the dining room. When they got set down to the table, Jim noticed that Louise cooked all the things that he liked. It was like a homecoming. The Allens were the closest thing he had to a family these days since his mother and sister still lived back East.

They had baked ham and sweet potatoes and sweet peas—and coffee, of course, since Louise knew that Jim preferred coffee for every meal. They had apple pie for dessert. And he could feel the warmth in the atmosphere. It was good to be around people who loved you.

After they had eaten, they resumed their musical concert. After Louise had done the dishes, she and Mr. Allen went to the living room and started dancing as they frequently did while their offspring and her man played music.

Jim played till his fingers hurt. Then Abe and Louise went off to bed, leaving the two young lovers alone on the couch. So Jim decided he had better fill Vickie in better on his plans for the next several months. He explained that he would need more horses. So he would probably go mustanging again. He said he had found several likely places where he could homestead some land since it wasn't settled yet. With the money he'd make from the drive, he should be able to have a nice ranch house built for her. And, of course, they'd have to have a barn and corral. With a cavvy of fifty or sixty saddle horses and a hundred or so broodmares, he'd have enough horses to start. And he had five hundred cows and twenty bulls already.

Vickie leaned against him, and he put his arms around her. "I just miss you *so* much when you're gone," she murmured.

"I miss you too," he said in turn. "But a man has to be able to make a living and provide for a family. You know I want our little ones to be well cared for." She grabbed his hand and squeezed it when he said that.

When it got late, Vickie walked him to their spare bedroom, so he went in and pulled off his clothes and turned in. It was the first time he had slept indoors in a bed for months. In fact, it was the first time he'd slept without his clothes on since the previous fall.

Trail Drive

Jim saddled up the next morning and rode out to find the herd. After leaving the Allen home, he was overcome with intense loneliness. It seemed that after being inside the Allen house, the rest of the world was cold and dreary in comparison. But the feeling gradually wore off. It would be hard not to enjoy the cool, crisp air and the bright sunshine and the wide, open spaces. The grass was green, and there were occasional bushes along the way.

He caught up with the herd at about noon. He saw the long line of longhorn critters with dust rising behind them. He rode on up until he saw the chuck wagon bouncing around alongside the long stream of cattle. It was nearly noon, so after a few minutes, the chuck wagon came to a halt. The cook and his flunky unhitched the team, then the cook hobbled them while the flunky started gathering wood for a fire. Jim dismounted and tied his horse to a wagon wheel. Bob, the flunky's name, didn't find enough wood lying around, so he got some wood out of the woodbox that was carried in the chuck wagon. Jim helped Bob start a fire, and the cook put on a pot of coffee to brew. In a few minutes, the coffee was ready, so Jim poured a cup and rolled a smoke while the two cooks cooked dinner.

With the herd moving, he knew they'd have to eat in shifts. So when Cookie called "Come and get it," he went to the tailgate of the wagon and filled up a plate and ate quickly so he could go relieve Joe and let him come in and eat. He saw clouds gathering in the sky, so he decided he'd better pull his slicker out of his saddlebag and tie it behind his saddle. He went to the chuck wagon, opened one of his saddlebags, and got it out. He didn't use his saddlebags while with the herd. He just left them in the chuck wagon. He tied his slicker to the pommel of his saddle.

The horse wrangler was a fifteen-year-old boy named Danny. Billy had drawn his wages and went back to his father's farm. The cook and cook's helper had rigged two ropes, with one end of each tied to the wagon wheel. Then they walked out away from the wagon on about a thirty-degree angle from each other, making a triangle of the two ropes. The cook's helper had tied two ropes together, so he still had a large coil of rope left when he and the cook stopped. When Danny hazed the horses up near the chuck wagon and into the triangle, he dismounted and took the coil of leftover rope from the cook's flunky and finished stringing it out so that it finished enclosing the triangle. He had left his own horse inside. There was still room for the horses to mill around.

As each cowboy rode up, Danny pulled back his end of the rope enough to make a gap in the makeshift corral for the cowboy to ride through. Each cowboy dismounted, unsaddled his horse, and turned him loose. He took his saddle and bridle and bent down to walk under the rope before laying his saddle down. Then he went to the fire to get grub. After he had eaten, he went back inside the rope triangle with his rope, roped a fresh horse, and saddled him. Then he mounted again, and Mark held the rope back for him to ride back out.

After Jim roped and saddled a fresh horse, he rode up to the point position to relieve Joe. "See Vickie?" Joe asked when Jim rode up to him. Redundant question, of course, but it was something to say.

"Yep," Jim replied. "You go eat. I'll take your spot here." The point riders rode point throughout the drive as did the swing riders. The flank and drag riders took turns. They were the least experienced men on the drive. They had hired more men in Killeen, where Cookie had stopped to buy up all the supplies he'd need for the trip. It wouldn't be long now before they'd reach the Red River. They'd crossed the Brazos about ten miles or so south of Waco.

After everyone had changed horses, Danny went to the fire and got himself a plate of grub. After ten minutes, he was through eating and went and roped a fresh horse and saddled hm. The cook's helper pulled the rope back so Danny could chase the horses out of his makeshift corral. Then he followed the horses as they ran off to find somewhere to graze. The cook's helper coiled the ropes back up, put them in the chuck wagon, and went to the fire to start water heating to wash dishes.

It was a cold, crisp day when they got up the following morning. They let the cattle graze when they first got up from their bedding ground. The cowboys all had breakfast, saddled their mounts, and rode out to relieve the night guard so they could come in and eat. Then, after the cows had grazed several hours, they got them moving north. It was April, so really hot weather hadn't set in yet. But it still got hot in the middle of the afternoon. One thing good about getting started this early in the season was that they should be one of the first herds to reach Abilene. So the herd might bring a better price for that reason.

As the afternoon wore on, clouds started gathering in the sky. It looked like it was about to rain. After about another thirty minutes, it did start raining. Jim reached down and untied his slicker from the pommel of his saddle and put it on without stopping. The rain cooled them off. It was a slow, drizzling rain. The cattle just kept on moving and didn't seem to mind the rain especially.

That evening, when they stopped for the night, the cook had to rig a tarp over the back of the chuck wagon because it was still raining. The men came by to get their plates and coffee cups filled up. There was beef and beans and corn bread. But the coffee was piping hot. The cook had a tarp rigged over the campfire nearby also to keep the rain from putting it out. He had driven four stakes in the ground around it to fasten it to. So they still had hot food.

Each cowboy had a tarp to lay over his bedroll so he could sleep dry. It was fairly dry anyway. It was hard to get rolled up in their blankets without getting a little wet. They had to do the best they could.

It was still raining the next morning. Each cowboy had to pull his boots on over damp socks. He put his boots inside his blankets and put them on before getting up. That was a little tricky because they always left their spurs fastened to their boots, but they managed. Then each cowboy put on his hat. A cowboy normally put his hat on first before his did his boots, but they made an exception this time. Then they went over to the fire for breakfast.

They normally let the cattle graze awhile before they started them moving. They weren't especially interested in grazing this morning. They wanted to turn their tails to the rain and drift. The wind was from the north, so it took some hooping and yelling and cussing to get them moving. They finally got the leaders of the herd to going into the wind, and the herd then followed.

At noon, the rain stopped, and the sun came out. The bright sun was a welcome sight. The cowboys removed their slickers and let the sun dry out their damp clothing. And the cattle started grazing. So there was some sense of order again. It was hard to estimate how far they went in a day, but Jim guessed that they still made about ten miles or so in spite of the rain.

They got the herd bedded down after supper and the night guards posted. The men that weren't on night guard bedded down. At midnight, it started raining again—just a light drizzling rain with no thunder or lightning. Jim was grateful for that. It was his turn to stand night guard, so he got out of his blankets, put on his hat, stamped on his boots, and donned his slicker. He was in a habit of keeping his night horse tied to a wagon wheel. All he had to do was tighten the cinch and mount up. When he got to the herd, he started singing as he always did. Had to keep the cattle quiet.

Come morning, the rain had stopped again, so the cook was able to get a fire going to cook breakfast without having to rig his tarp. The cattle started grazing as soon as they got up like normal. Jim decided they were getting along pretty well all in all.

Jim and Jack took turns scouting ahead. Jim had the experience of making one drive to Kansas. Jack had the experience of making several to Saint Louis. So Jim knew the route better than Jack. He had noticed that Jack had more trail savvy than he. They put Joe and

Sam to riding point, and they spent most of their time scouting the territory ahead so they wouldn't have any surprises.

While the cattle were grazing the next morning, Jim heard several shots ring out. He went over to investigate. Several cows had calved that morning, so the cowboys had shot the calves. No way they could keep up. They had left the young cows behind, but they had included some old cows. And old cows can still calve for several years after they get old.

"Why can't we skin out the calves and have fresh veal for chuck?" Sam asked.

Jim and Jack both liked the idea. So the next time Jack shot a calf, he waited until the angry mother settled down, then leaned out of the saddle, grabbed one leg of the dead calf, pulled it up, and laid it across his pommel. Then he took it to the chuck wagon. He dropped it and told the cook's flunky to skin it out and butcher it. It took several calves just to make enough meat for one meal for the number of cowboys that they had to feed. They had a mixed reaction about the quality of meat. Some of the cowboys thought it was really delicious. But there were other cowboys that preferred the taste of the full beef. They still ate it without complaint.

Then, one morning, shortly after the men had saddled up to go look after the herd, a woman came riding up in a wagon. She looked like she was in her early twenties and had a little boy who appeared to be about four or five years old in the seat beside her. She drove up to the chuck wagon.

"Do you have any baby calves?" she asked the cook.

"Yes, we're having a few calves born," he answered.

"Can I have them?" she asked.

"You'll have to ask one of our trail bosses" was his answer. One of the riders was within sight of the chuck wagon. The cook waved at him to come over. He rode on over. It was a young greenie named Allen. "Go get Jim or Jack and ask them to ride over to the chuck wagon," he told him.

So Jim rode up to the chuck wagon and saw the young woman and little boy setting in the wagon. He could tell she was a fine-looking woman though she had a bonnet that shaded her face.

"Can I have any baby calves that you don't want?" she asked.

"Sure," he said. He told Allen to pass the word around to all the boys not to shoot any more calves but to just bring them into the chuck wagon instead. He found out the woman's name was Jill and her little boy was named Jacob.

By noon, they had half a dozen baby calves loaded into her wagon. The cook's flunky tied their feet so they couldn't get up and jump out. She told them thanks and drove off. That evening, just before chuck, she was back. This time, she had five pies in the back of the wagon. She had them packed in a box with cardboard between them to keep them from getting jumbled up—apple pies. She was invited to have supper with them. She was a very pleasant woman to talk to. She was a brunette with green eyes. A nice build as far as you could see with the modest long dress she was wearing. And it showed some wear. It was faded and patched in a few places.

"What have you got, a herd of dairy cows?" a cowboy named Ben asked during supper.

"I have a herd of milk goats" was her answer. "So this way, I won't have to milk them. One mama goat can raise a calf."

When she left to go back home, she had another five baby calves in the back of her wagon.

"She's probably a war widow," Jack ventured after she left. "That war left a lot of young widows behind." Ben was standing at Jack's elbow.

"A mighty good-looking woman," Ben said.

"You could probably go calling sometime after we get back," Jack said. "I'll bet she's lonesome."

When they approached the Red River, they found it flooded. The muddy water was washing up over the banks. The water was racing downstream fiercely, and there were lots of brush and tree trunks being carried along. No way could they swim the cattle across it.

Jack suggested to Jim, "If you follow the river to the west looking for a good place to cross, I'll do the same to the east."

"Sounds like a good idea," Jim said and turned his horse to the west. He kept on riding and riding. The river was flooding its banks in places, and the water was rushing downstream rapidly. There were a lot of branches, brush, and logs from downed trees floating down. Jim rode half a day and never found a likely place to cross. He wound up missing dinner. He got hungry but kept on riding. When his horse got thirsty, he could find a place where he could get a drink; but he hadn't brought his canteen, so he just endured the thirst himself. He returned to the chuck wagon that evening to learn from Jack that he never found a place to cross either. They'd have to just hold the herd until the river went down a little. Jim went to the water bucket and drank a couple of dippers full of water before he poured himself a cup of coffee. Then he got a plate full of food.

It was another four days before the river went down enough to take the cattle across. They couldn't find a place to ford it but found a place they thought they could swim the cattle across fairly easily. They unhitched the team from the chuck wagon, tied the tongue of it up so it wouldn't hit the bottom, and just had two cowboys fasten a rope to each side and pull it across behind their swimming horses. Then Jim ordered Danny to swim the horses across next. When Danny finished getting the horses up the far bank, they got the leaders of the herd into the water and got them to swimming. The herd was restless due to the inactivity of the last few days. It was easier than usual to get the cattle moving into the water and to swimming. After a couple of hours, they had all the cattle across too. They were now in Indian country.

CHAPTER 19

Comanches and Rustlers

Once they were north of the Red River, Jim said to Jack, "We'd better be alert for another Indian attack." Jack had made several drives to Missouri but hadn't made a drive to Abilene yet. So he hadn't traveled this exact route.

Jim explained further, "This is the same point on the route where the Indians attacked last fall. I think we'd better double the guard on the horses. And every man, while sleeping, should keep a horse saddled and tied."

"Yep, I agree to that except I think we should triple the guard on the horses. That's mainly what the Indians will go after."

So that night, each cowboy tied a saddled horse either to one of the wheels of the chuck wagon or to a tree or bush near where he was sleeping.

They generally had four men guarding the cattle and one man guarding the horses. The men guarding the cattle would ride around the herd and sing to them sweet and low to keep them calmed down. So with three men guarding the horses, they had seven men on guard at a time. They had eighteen men along on the drive. And, of course, the cook and the flunky didn't have to stand night guard. So they had half the men on guard the first half of the night while the other half tried to get some sleep. Then they changed the guard so the other half of the crew could get some sleep.

Jim decided to take his turn at guard duty the last half of the night as usual. He thought the likelihood of Indian attack was greatest then, like before. Jack took his turn the first half of the night. He thought it was best to have an experienced Indian fighter on each shift.

Jim went on guard at midnight. He had gone to bed at 8:00 p.m.—four hours of sleep. They'd be getting up at 4:00 a.m. to get breakfast and let the herd start grazing. And he started hearing quail calls as soon as he went out and relieved Jack. He knew what that meant. Quail weren't likely to be calling unless something had disturbed them. And he had heard nothing that would disturb them. So either something was prowling about soundlessly or it wasn't quail doing the calling.

At about three o'clock, he saw a dark form approaching the horse herd. He turned his horse toward it. Then he saw feathers sticking out of the horse's mane. He was carrying his Henry across his saddle and immediately brought it up and fired. He shot the Indian out of the saddle. The horses immediately stampeded as did the cattle. So the running fight with the Indians had started. There was no moon, but it was a clear night. He could see the Indian ponies by starlight just like he had in the previous Indian fight with the Comanches last fall. He just fired at every paint horse he saw. He thought again of the Indian trick of riding on the side of his horse and shooting at the cowboys from under their pony's neck. So he just shot the Indian's horses out from under them whenever he spotted them. Gunfire erupted all around him as the other cowboys did the same.

The Indians tried to get between the horses and the cattle so they could turn them, but Jim was ready for that. He especially kept his attention on the gap between the horses and cattle and kept shooting Indians every time he saw one of them try to ride into that gap. When his rifle went empty, he took cartridges out of his vest pocket and reloaded it quickly with his horse still in a full gallop.

He felt a bullet whiz by his ear and saw the flash of the shot. He pulled up his rifle and shot at it. Not likely to hit anything while in a full gallop unless you're really close, but he figured the Indian had the same trouble. He saw the flash again and pulled his horse to a halt. The next time he saw the flash, he fired directly at it. Then he got his horse moving again. The Indian didn't shoot back this time, so he figured he got him. So there's traders trading guns to the Indians in this part of the country too! Either that or it was guns the Indians had managed to steal in some fight.

He didn't really know how long the fight lasted. The noise of the stampeding herd drowned out the sound of gunfire. He just reached the point that he noticed that they were chasing the stampeding critters and saw no more paint horses.

The cattle kept running till the gray of daylight started showing in the east before they finally got them to milling. After the cowboys got the cattle and horses settled down, they rode out around the herd to see if there was any further sign of the attackers. There was none. They wouldn't know if they got away with any horses until it got light enough to count them.

They came in four at a time to get chuck after Cookie got breakfast ready. Then they changed horses and got the herd moving. After running all night, they'd want to bed down. Jim knew they wouldn't graze as tired as they were, but they wanted to get them away from the area. They'd let them graze that afternoon if they wanted to. They should be hungry after they calmed down a little. They didn't really want them to bed down during the day. They'd want to be up all night again if they did.

That evening, they finally stopped for the night, and they permitted the cattle to bed down. Cookie called, "Come and git it," so they posted a regular guard of four cowboys to guard the herd in addition to one for the horses. The other cowboys gratefully came in to eat. So the greenies had gotten some experience Indian fighting. They'd no longer be greenies by the time they reached Abilene.

Jack and Jim scouted ahead as usual. They left Joe and Sam riding point again. They were about two hundred yards apart and in and out of trees. There was a trail of sorts that led through the trees so the cattle would be able to keep moving without too much difficulty. Jim saw some dust ahead, so he knew there were riders coming.

Jim headed toward where he thought Jack would be and, after a few minutes, saw him coming toward him.

"Riders up ahead," Jim mused as he rode up to Jack and slowed down to ride beside him.

"Yep. And from the dust I see, there must be a lot of them. We'd better ride back to the herd and get ready for them."

"It would be good if one of us rode up without letting them see us so we can see how many they are and get an idea of their intentions."

"It better be both of us. It isn't good to have just one man up against them," Jack answered.

"Then the men with the herd wouldn't know what's going on," Jim told him his thought.

"I'll ride ahead. I did a lot of scouting during the war. I won't let them see me," Jack said.

So Jim wheeled his horse and spurred him toward the herd. He had him run for all he was worth. When he reached Joe and Sam, he told them, "Start the herd milling. There's riders up ahead." The trail was wide enough at this point that this was possible. "Then I want the following riders to leave the herd and come with me." And he named off the names of the riders he wanted. His horse was in a lather by then, so he rode over to the horse cavvy, roped a horse, and changed saddles. The men he had named off were riding up by then.

"There's riders up ahead. We're going up to meet them. And I want John, Badger, Gill, Don, and Able to ride into the trees maybe a hundred yards or so to the left side of the riders, dismount, have your rifles drawn, and each one of you get behind a tree. You'll open fire if I move my arm like this." And he lifted his arm and pulled it down swiftly. "The rest of you come with me." Then he spurred his horse and started back up to the trail to where he thought the riders would be by now.

Where is Jack? Jim thought as they waited for the riders to ride up. Then he saw the riders, and they had their rifles out too. They held up when they saw Jim and his men.

"State your business," Jim said as he held his rifle across the pommel of his saddle. It wouldn't take a second to raise it and fire it.

"We're looking for a stolen herd," he said.

"We have a herd of cattle, but they aren't stolen," Jim replied.

"We want to cut your herd and see," the stranger said.

"What brand are you looking for?" was Jim's question.

"Circle S."

"We do have some Circle S strays in the herd but not many. A couple of dozen maybe. You can have them," Jim then said.

"We'll cut your whole herd," the strange rider then said. Jim knew that if the men stampeded the cattle in these trees, it would take days to get them gathered back up again, and if these men were rustlers, they'd gather as many of them as they could too.

"No go. If you'll turn around and ride back to where you came from there is a cleared area after about ten miles or so. You can watch the cattle go by, and you'll see there aren't but about twenty-five or so steers with a Circle S brand."

Jim saw him bring his rifle up, and he reined his horse to the right and pulled his own rifle up. He felt the bullet go by just where he had been. He fired his rifle, but it missed. The stranger had reined his horse out of the way too. Jim raised his left arm and brought it down.

There was a staccato of rifle fire from the trees to Jim's left. Jim turned a somersault and left his saddle just as another bullet whizzed by barely above his saddle horn. Jim lay down on the ground, levered another shell into his rifle, and fired at one of the rustlers. He saw him drop from the saddle. He saw men falling from their saddles as the bullets from the trees found their targets. He saw the leader, on the ground this time, and fired at him. His bullet found its target this time.

The rest of the rustlers wheeled their horses and rode off. Jim looked for his horse. He was fifty feet or so away. He walked over to him and mounted.

There were probably seven or eight dead bodies on the ground.

Then Jack rode up. "We'd better follow them and make sure they don't lay for us again," he said.

"Their leader is dead. We might not have any more trouble from them," Jim said.

Two of the men did catch a bullet. John had caught a bullet in the side, but the bullet went on through. Jim took some bandages from his saddlebag and bandaged it up. Gill had a graze on his arm. Jim and Jack agreed to care for their own wounded first. While Jim was putting a bandage on John's arm, Jack bandaged Gill's wound. They would have to wait for the chuck wagon to catch up and load John onto the chuck wagon because he couldn't ride.

"There is a place up ahead where they can hide in rocks and stampede our cattle into the woods as the herd goes by. It would take days to get them bunched back into a herd and the rustlers could help themselves to all the cattle they wanted in the process," Jim said.

"But if we turn the herd around and go south until we get clear of the trees, we can go around them and the rustlers will be waiting for nothing," Jim went on.

So they left one man behind watching the wounded and rode back to the chuck wagon. They explained to the cook where the wounded men were and gave him instructions to go up, pick up Gill and John, and then come back. Jim explained, "The herd will be heading south now."

CHAPTER 20

Thirsty Cattle

They moved the cattle south until they reached the rolling prairie again, then headed them east.

"This route will take us into Kiowa country," Jim said that night at the campfire.

"Yes," said Jack.

"And we'll be delayed from reaching the Canadian River, which was planned to be our next water hole," said Jim.

"Yes, we'll have to go longer without water than we planned."

But they had saved their herd from the rustlers, so they still had their cattle. They kept the herd heading east until they were clear of the wooded area. It would be a disaster to have a stampede to deal with in those trees. It would have taken them days to get the herd bunched up and moving as a herd again.

Gill's wound was minor enough that he insisted that he could ride. They put him to riding flank. That would be better than riding drag, they thought. John still had to ride in the chuck wagon.

You could tell that the cattle were getting restless. They had planned to be at the Canadian River by now so they could drink. But now there was no water. When they reached the point that there was nothing but rolling prairie to the north, they turned the cattle and got them heading toward the river. There was a slight breeze from the southwest, so the cattle couldn't smell the water yet.

But their luck couldn't hold out forever. The wind shifted around to blow from the north, and the leaders of the herd got the scent of water. They immediately started running. Within minutes, there was a full stampede in progress. The men just ran their horses alongside the cattle and let them go. There was nothing else they could do.

It was several hours before they reached the river. When it looked like they were getting close, the cowboys rode farther away from the cattle, hoping they'd spread out a little. When they reached the river, the cattle never slowed down until they hit the water. They couldn't drink because of the cattle crowding behind them, shoving them deeper into the river.

It was mass confusion, but the cattle that were in too deep of water to stop and drink just swam the river and quenched their thirst in the shallow water on the far side.

They did get the cattle all watered and across the river before nightfall.

The next morning, they got the herd to heading north again. They had several days of nothing but their daily routine. The weather turned fair. It was early enough in the spring that it was still cool. Jim and Jack took turns scouting ahead. They left Joe and Sam riding point, and they rode ahead together. If there was any likelihood of danger, it was better to have two men together rather than just one. When they approached Kiowa country, they decided they had better scout together. They expected they'd have an encounter with the Kiowa tribe.

And sure enough, when Jim and Jack rode ahead to make sure the way was clear for the herd, they saw what looked like a hundred Kiowa warriors formed up in a line waiting for them. They boldly rode up to what looked like the Kiowa chief and halted in front of him. Neither of them spoke Kiowa, but Jack knew the universal sign language that all Indians used. He signaled his greeting to the chief, and the chief signaled a greeting in return. The chief explained he wanted two hundred cattle in return for crossing his land.

"Too many," Jack answered in sign language. "He said he wants two hundred head," he told Jim.

The chief's hands moved in a fashion that Jim didn't understand, of course. Jack said, "He said that we can't cross his land then."

Jim just sat his saddle with his rifle across the pommel and watched. The conversation between the chief and Jack continued, but of course, Jim couldn't tell what the chief and Jack were saying. They obviously were bickering. Finally, they concluded their conversation, and Jack turned to Jim and said, "He says he'll accept twenty head of steers in return for safe passage across his land. I agreed to give them to him. Except don't cut out scrubs. Pick out good steers. I told him we'd give him good beef."

So Jack remained with the chief while Jim rode back to the herd to tell the men to cut out twenty head of steers to give to the Indians. And he told them, "Pick out good quality steers with some tallow on them. But pick out strays if you can."

They started the cattle to milling, and then two of the boys cut out twenty head of the stray steers that had joined the herd. Jim noticed that most of them were Circle S steers. He started them moving back to the place where Jack and the Indians were waiting.

When the chief saw the cattle that Jim had brought him, he was satisfied. They were good quality cattle with plenty of tallow. So he and his braves moved around the steers and headed them toward their village. Jim rode back to tell the men to get the herd moving again.

They were only about a week from Abilene. They had two more rivers to cross. Then they would be within a day's ride. Neither of the rivers were flooding, so crossing them turned out to be fairly easy.

After they got past the second river, Jack and Jim rode ahead to find a buyer. Before they found a buyer, they found a law officer. He came riding toward them before they reached the town.

"You'll have to turn your guns in before riding into town," he told them.

Jack replied with "I'll have the boys leave their guns at the chuck wagon. They won't argue about that near as much as they would about leaving them at your office"

"That will be satisfactory. But if you want to ride into town, you'll have to leave your guns at my office for now."

"Okay," Jack said.

They rode with the marshal to his office, removed their gun belts, took them and their rifles inside, and left them on the marshal's desk. Then they asked the marshal where they could find a buyer for the herd. He told them they'd probably find him at the hotel.

They found a buyer in the restaurant drinking coffee. He was dressed in a broadcloth suit and had a top hat lying on the table. He had a gray beard and gray hair, but he was slender built.

"I'm Jack Watkins, and this is Jim Bennett," he told them.

"Mack Newberry," the buyer said.

"We have a herd to sell," Jack then told him.

"I do buy cattle. I want to look at them first."

"Can you meet us about ten miles south of the town?" asked Jack.

"Sure. How about ten o'clock tomorrow morning?"

They rode over to the marshal's office, retrieved their guns, and mounted up again, heading back to the herd. When they reached the chuck wagon, they told the cook to set up camp, and then they halted the herd about ten miles from town as they had arranged with the buyer.

At the campfire that night, Jack explained to the boys that they had to leave their guns in the chuck wagon before riding into town.

"I have to have my gun," Gill said. "What if someone called you liar?" They always killed anyone that called them a liar—unless he killed them first.

"Whoever calls you a liar won't have a gun either," Jack said.

None of the men liked the idea.

"The alternative is to leave them at the marshal's office," Jack explained. "I figured leaving them at the chuck wagon would be better than that."

The following morning, the buyer rode up. He noticed the rangy-looking cowboys. None of them had had a shave in six weeks. The only time they got a bath or did laundry was when they had to swim a river. "We'll need a count of the herd. I can look at them while we are counting them," he told them.

The cook and the cook's flunky were quartering out a steer they had just skinned. They were running low on meat for the cook's fire.

They hadn't taken a tally of the cow critters since they had left Texas. So Jim gave orders to the cowboys to start the herd moving in a circle with the buyer on one side with Jack sitting his horse beside him and Jim on the other side. It took about an hour to make their count. The buyer counted 2,423, and Jim counted 2,420. So they accepted the buyer's count. They settled on a price of twenty-eight dollars per head. The cattle had put on quite a bit of tallow on the drive. The grass had greened up good because it was spring. But $67,844 sounded like a lot of money to Jim. Of course, they had to pay the men and buy supplies for the return trip. And they had to pay back Sam for his initial investment, and the remaining profit had to be split four ways.

They headed the herd toward town to load them into the stock pens. After they had the herd in the pens, Jim told the men, "Ride on back to the chuck wagon for now. That's where you'll get your pay. After you get paid, you can ride on into town."

CHAPTER 21

Abilene

They were eager to go into town of course. The four partners accompanied the buyer over to the hotel, where he wrote them a check. Then Jack and Jim rode over to the saloon where they knew the marshal would be and walked up to him.

"We need to bring our guns into town," Jim told him.

"And why?" Marshall Will asked him.

"We are going to the bank to cash our check so we can pay the men," Jim answered.

"I especially *don't* want you taking your guns into the bank" was the marshal's answer.

"And what's to prevent someone from robbing us the instant we leave the bank?" asked Jack.

"My boys will escort you from the bank to your chuck wagon" was the marshal's explanation.

So the four partners went to a dry goods store first so each could buy a money belt before going to the bank. When they arrived at the bank, they saw four deputies waiting outside at the hitch rail. They went into the bank.

After cashing their check, Jack put the money they'd need to pay the men and buy supplies into a canvas sack. He also took out the money that Sam had loaned them to pay wages and buy supplies during the trip and put it in a separate sack. Then he divided the rest four ways. They put the money in their money belts and slipped them inside their shirts and buckled them before leaving the bank. The four deputies rode with them back to the chuck wagon.

The men all lined up except for the horse wrangler to get their pay. The horse wrangler was still watching the horses. One and a half month's pay amounted to $67.50 for each cowboy. Jack had drawn gold and silver dollars to pay the men with. Each one got three double eagles and seven silver dollars and a fifty-cent piece. The cook's pay was seventy-five dollars a month. So one and half month's pay for him was $112.50. And of course, Jack gave Sam the separate sack with the money owed to him.

Then Jack rode out and relieved the horse wrangler so he could get his pay. Jim volunteered to take the first turn at watching the horses so the horse wrangler could ride into town too. The men didn't have their guns; so they couldn't fire them into the air when they rode down the streets of Abilene, but they made up for it with yelling.

The bathhouses and barbershops did a booming business at first. The men were all eager to get a bath, a haircut, and a shave. Some of them stopped by the dry goods store to buy a new shirt if the one they were wearing was too worn or ragged. Then they headed for the nearest saloon. After Jack, Joe, and Sam had gotten cleaned up and had a good meal at the restaurant, Jack rode out to the horse herd to relieve Jim. So Jim managed to a get a bath, a shave, and a haircut too. Joe and Sam went to a saloon. Jim didn't drink, so after he'd had a meal at the restaurant, he rode back out to the chuck wagon to relieve Jack again so he could ride into town and wet his whistle.

Of course, the first thing Jim did when he got back was to stop at the chuck wagon and put on his gun belt and retrieve his rifle. He didn't want to ride around naked any longer than he had to.

Jack was back from town at about midnight and took over the horse guard so that Jim could roll up in his blankets and get some sleep. He had the same feeling as Jim about his guns. He picked them up at the chuck wagon before riding out to relieve Jim. Jim relieved Jack again at 4:00 a.m. since he knew he hadn't had any sleep yet.

The cook had breakfast ready for them at about six. So Jack got up to eat breakfast kind of red-eyed but cheerful.

The payroll amounted to over $900. They needed about $200 for supplies for the return trip. But they hadn't sold any horses yet. And they intended to sell all the horses except their best cow horses. It took too long to train a cow horse. Horses were a much better price in Abilene than in Texas, so it was practical to sell all but the best horses and just buy more horses when they got back to Texas.

Jack rode into town and found a horse buyer to ride out and look at the horses they wanted to sell. He didn't turn in his guns to the marshal, and the marshal didn't bother him about it. The horse buyer rode out with Jack to look at the horses. Jim had cut out the horses they wanted to keep and put them into a different bunch. It turned out they had forty-two head of horses for the buyer to look at. They settled on a price of forty dollars a head. So that was another $1,680. The horse buyer paid them in cash.

*****

Jim rode into town again to let the men know they were heading back to Texas. He figured the first place to look would be the saloon. He tied his horse at the rail and walked in. He saw Gil and Barry sitting at a table playing cards.

Jim walked over and said, "Do you know where the rest of the men are at?"

"Zeke and Al are in jail," answered Gil, looking up from his cards. "They got in a fight and were wrecking furniture and such. The marshal arrested them. I guess the rest of them are probably at the Wary Eagle or one of the other saloons."

"Do you want to ride back to Texas with us?" Jim then asked.

"I do," said Gil.

"Me too," echoed Barry.

"Okay. Then be back at the chuck wagon by tomorrow morning." So Jim left, mounted his horse, and rode over to the jail. He walked in and found Pete, the jailer, sitting at the desk.

"I understand that you have two of my men in jail," he said to Pete.

"Which ones are they?" Pete asked.

"Zeke and Al."

"Yes, they're back there. The marshal arrested them for fighting and wrecking furniture. They were drunk, of course, but being drunk ain't against the law. Wrecking the property of others is."

"What will it take for me to get them out?" Jim asked.

"Just pay their fines and pay for the property they destroyed," Pete answered.

Jim learned that their fines were twenty dollars each and the furniture they wrecked totaled to another thirty dollars. So Jim paid the jailer seventy dollars. Pete went back and let them out of their cell.

"When we get back to Texas, you can work out the cost of your fines and damage to property if you work for me," Jim told them.

"I'll do that," said Zeke somewhat sheepishly.

"Me too," said Al.

Jim knew they would. Both men were honest. They just didn't hold their liquor very well. Jim told them to get their horses from the hostler and gave them the money to pay the hostler his bill. Then he went to saloon after saloon until he found all the men. There were another six cowboys that wanted to ride back with them. That made ten in all. So he rode back to the camp and told the cook to take the chuck wagon into town to get supplies. After he came back, they bunched up the horse cavvy and headed south toward Texas again the last week in May.

Sam had about $4,000 in all from the money he had loaned them during the drive in addition to his share of the profits. So he had over $19,000 in his money belt.

Jim's share of the profit was just over $15,000. He just divided it into two canvas sacks and put it in his saddlebags. Since most of it was gold, it wouldn't fit in his money belt. He would have deposited it in the bank, but there were no stage lines between Abilene and Waco and no telegraph either. So he couldn't have it transferred to a

Waco bank. Besides, somebody might rob the bank. That happened occasionally.

He had spent only about twenty dollars or so getting cleaned up and having a good meal. He took time out to go to a jewelry store to buy a set of wedding rings for Vickie. That cost him $1,000. But he still had nearly $14,000 in gold in his saddlebags when they left for Texas. He kept some of the money in his pocket just for traveling expenses.

So Jim figured he had enough money to start his ranch now. The next morning, Jim, Jack, the cook, the cook's helper, and ten cowboys left Abilene and headed south back toward Texas. They had brought along the horses they didn't want to sell. Joe and Sam stayed behind. They liked to go to saloons, and Sam liked to gamble.

The 4-C crew had kept their chuck wagon and the cook had provisioned it with plenty of supplies before leaving Abilene. So they enjoyed the good food that the cook was so good at putting together. Since Cookie had just killed a steer before they sold the herd, they had plenty of fresh beef.

They would be back in Indian country again soon, so they doubled the guard on the horses at night. More herds would be headed up the Chisholm Trail. So they figured the Indians' attention would be diverted to some degree by the new herds coming up. What Jim wanted was to get through Indian country while drawing the minimum amount of attention.

As they rode, Jim noticed dust in the distance ahead. So there must be a crew that left before they did. Not unusual though; they hadn't seen anyone leaving before they left the bank and headed to their chuck wagon.

By midmorning, the dust was no longer visible. Now Jim wondered about that. If there was another trail drive crew that had just left Abilene, they should still see their dust.

Jim rode up alongside of Jack, "Did you see some dust coming up from the horizon a couple of hours ago?"

"Yep. And it's gone now," Jack said.

"So there were riders ahead of us."

"And they aren't moving now."

"Indians maybe?" Jim asked.

"Probably not Indians. They'd either approach us and want something for passage through their land or just attack us and try to steal our horses," Jack answered.

"So maybe white men. Robbers, huh?"

"Could be," said Jack.

"If they have an ambush set up ahead of us and we changed our path of travel, they couldn't ambush us then."

"Nope," answered Jack.

So Jim rode over to the chuck wagon and told the cook to change their direction of travel to the right. There wasn't a trail. Just rolling prairie. They changed their direction to the southwest. At noon, they stopped, and the men gathered up some cow chips for a fire. The cook had some wood and kindling in the woodbox on the wagon to get the fire started. Then he added the cow chips. The cook's helper started peeling potatoes, and the cook started slicing some steaks from a slab of beef into a skillet.

Jim saw some dust again to the east. The cowboys had all loosened their cinches and hobbled their horses. They had poured themselves coffee and were sitting around the fire.

"Everyone, tighten your cinches and unhobble your horses," Jim ordered. "We have company coming."

The cook started reharnessing the team and got them ready to move. He headed toward a wooded area that would be easier to defend. The cook did take the coffeepot off the fire just before he jumped up into the wagon seat and started the chuck wagon moving.

And just in time. The riders appeared over the rise shooting as they came. Each cowboy yanked his rifle from its boot, dismounted, tied his horse to a tree, and got behind it. They started returning their fire. The horse cavvy stampeded, of course.

The attackers dismounted too. They got behind soapweed bushes from just over the rise both in front, behind, and on both sides. Some of them found rocks to hide behind. There must have been two dozen men shooting at them from all sides. They were surrounded!

"After our gold," Jack murmured as he jacked a shell into the chamber of his rifle.

"Yes. Apparently a band of robbers. Someone must have told them we were carrying gold," said Jim. "Or maybe some of them saw us leaving the bank." Jim still had his gold in his saddlebags, the same with Jack. The rest of the cowboys would have their pay either in their pockets or in a money belt. That's if they hadn't lost it all playing cards. Jack's horse was tied to a tree as was Jim's, but they were penned down by the gunfire.

Well, it wasn't good being surrounded. And the horses had been stampeded. They'd steal them for sure.

CHAPTER 22

Gamblers

Meanwhile, back in Abilene, Joe and Sam were having the time of their lives. They were wearing new clothes and had a bath and a shave every morning. Then went to a restaurant and had a breakfast of bacon and eggs. The first morning after Jack and Jim left with the cowboys, they sat down to eat. They both ordered a dozen fried eggs with ham and biscuits. The waitress was a pretty girl with dark-brown hair and amber-colored eyes.

When Joe saw her approach, he stood up and bowed to her. "Good morning, fair damsel," he said. "It is so good to see so much beauty this early in the day."

She blushed and paused a moment to regain her composure. When she finally thought she had her face straight again, she asked, "What do you want to order?"

Joe ordered half a dozen eggs and pancakes this time with bacon. Sam did the same. They both watched her walk all the way back to the kitchen to turn in their order.

Joe was still just feeling good having money in his pocket again. He had been broke for so long. Sam had loaned money to the partnership on several occasions and had been reimbursed. So he had even more money than Joe. Joe had put most of his money in the bank but still had plenty to pay expenses with and some left to spend on cards and drink. Sam had all his money in his money belt around his waist under his shirt.

They had several cups of coffee while waiting for their breakfast to cook. When the waitress came back with their breakfast, Joe winked at her, and she blushed again. The waitress seemed to be about five foot two and was obviously well-built. She had on a floor-length dress, of course, but it fit snug above the waist. So you could tell she was a shapely lass.

"What might your name be?" asked Joe while she was placing their food on the table.

"It might be Sally, but it isn't," she answered. She finished placing their food on the table and turned and walked off. She only came by their table to refill their coffee cups when needed, topped off their coffee, and turned and disappeared again. The restaurant had filled up with customers, so this was understandable. But she also was apparently avoiding them—a smart girl.

After they had finished eating, they paid their bill and headed over to the Wary Eagle. It was ten o'clock in the morning, but it was open. Saloons opened early when the trail herds started arriving in Abilene.

They walked in and ordered coffee from the bartender. It was still a little too early for a drink. But they thought they might find a friendly little game.

Then two men came in. They had the look of a professional gambler about them with their broadcloth suits and ruffled white shirts. They walked over to a table, and before they sat down, they looked toward Joe and Sam and said, "Anyone interested in a friendly little game?" Joe and Sam both walked over and sat down with them. The one who invited them over introduced himself as Walt and his companion as Rob.

Walt asked the bartender for a new deck of cards. Then he shuffled them and laid the deck down for Joe to cut the pack. Joe did so, and Walt dealt the cards. So the game began. Before long, a bar girl came by in a dress with bare shoulders and lots of ruffles in the skirt. One side of the skirt was tied up with a red bow at the knee. You rarely ever got a look at anything above a girl's ankle. She came to see if they wanted a drink. All of them ordered. Joe's eyes followed her as she walked away.

The game continued and the girl, who gave her name as Flo, came by every time their glasses got empty to see if they wanted more drinks. They ordered again each time.

At first, Joe and Sam won steadily but with small pots. Then Sam won a big pot. He suggested they increase the table limit. The other three agreed. Sam won another hand. Then he lost one. Then won another. He suggested they increase the limit again, and Rob seemed reluctant; but Walt said, "Our luck will surely change," so Rob agreed. Then Rob won a big pot. He obviously felt better after that.

Then Joe's and Sam's luck seemed to turn sour. They lost four large pots in a row. Then Joe won one. But as the game continued, Joe and Sam started losing steadily. When Joe was broke, he tossed in his cards. He wasn't really broke because he had put most of his money in the bank. But he'd used all the money he had on him. So Joe moved to the bar, taking his drink with him.

Sam continued in the game. But by the middle of the afternoon, he was broke too. Then Joe saw him reach over and hit Walt's hand really hard and hold it to the table. Sam had a gorilla grip, and try as he might, Walt couldn't pull free. Then Sam turned over the gambler's hand. It held an ace. Four aces had already been played. It seemed like bringing a fifth ace into the game was a common gambler trick. When Sam went for his gun, he saw the gambler's gun was already leveling on him. It looked like he had gotten his gun out too late, but just before the gambler fired, he heard a shot, and Walt fell against the table. The other gambler was reaching for his gun. Another shot rang out, and he slumped against the table too and then slid to the floor. Sam glanced toward Joe and saw he held a smoking gun. They heard yelling in the street. Joe rushed out the door. Sam quickly put as much of the money from the table as he could in his pockets before rushing out the saloon hall door too. They ran out, hurried to their horses, and mounted up, spurring their horses to a sprint to get out of town.

They knew of the marshal's rule that no guns were allowed in town. But when they had ridden to the chuck wagon to pick up their gear just before the 4-C crew left, they brought their guns back with them. They figured if the marshal didn't know about it, it wouldn't hurt him.

They rode south from the town for a full hour before they stopped and walked their horses awhile to let them catch their breath. Then they started them going again at a comfortable gallop. After half an hour or so, they turned and looked and saw dust rising from the direction of town. They spurred their horses and got them to running hard again. They first had to outrun the posse and then figure out a way to lose them.

They were headed straight for Indian country. They didn't know if the posse would follow them that far or not. But for now, they had to push on. The horses they were riding were in good shape. They were used to being ridden hard for several hours at a time every few days. Sure, they'd wear out, but the posse's horses would wear out too.

After a couple of hours, Joe looked back and saw that the posse was falling behind. They kept up their pace until the dust from the posse behind them disappeared over the horizon, then they slowed their horses to a walk. They knew the posse would have to do the same pretty soon or they'd kill their horses.

They kept riding until after it was dark. They kept their horses at a walk but kept going until it was about midnight. They could tell the time pretty close just by looking at the Big Dipper.

They finally found a place to camp near a creek. They were exhausted as were the horses. They were also thirsty. They drank their fill from the creek and let the horses drink. Then they unsaddled and picketed their horses and rolled up in their bedrolls, which they always kept tied behind their saddles. They had no food but were too exhausted to notice. They went to sleep almost instantly.

At the first gray light of dawn, they saddled up and were riding again. Five hours of rest had worked wonders for both man and beast, but Joe and Sam were both now aware of being very hungry. And they wished they had some coffee. The sun finished coming up, and they stopped periodically to study their back trail. No sign of dust. So maybe the posse had turned back. It was too soon to tell. But in the middle of the afternoon, they saw a plume of dust rising from the horizon in front of them. They didn't see any way the posse could have gotten in front. They pushed on, hoping they wouldn't kill their spent horses.

Then they heard gunfire up ahead! They spurred their horses and galloped on to see what was going on! They saw some horses that were obviously stampeding, and Joe recognized several of the horses in their own cavvy. He saw Jim's buckskin running past.

Then, when riding over a rise, they saw a clump of trees and saw men hiding in the soapweed shooting at some other men that were hiding in a clump of trees. They recognized the chuck wagon nearby.

They immediately pulled their rifles from their saddle boots, and Joe fired at one of the gunmen just ahead. Then he reined his horse to the left, stopped, and jacked in another round into the chamber of his rifle all in one motion. They he fired at another. Sam saw what he was doing and did likewise.

The bandits found themselves in a crossfire. But by moving back and forth in between shots, Joe and Sam were making it look like they were a lot more than just two men. Sam found he could move his horse to just up over the rise, fire, then turn him back to get below the rise, jack a shell into his rifle, move his horse either to the right or left, come just over the rise another time, and fire again. With Joe and him doing the same, it looked like they were attacking them with a major force.

The bandits immediately ran for their horses, mounted, and headed out—the ones that were still alive at least. There were several lying on the ground dead.

Then Joe and Sam fired several shots after the retreating riders, then attacked the ones in the soapweed on the left flank.

Jim and Jack's crew concentrated their fire now on the attackers on their right flank, and there were still bandits shooting at them from behind. But the bandits mistakenly concluded they were out-numbered, and all of them mounted up and left.

Then Joe and Sam rode down to the clump of bushes where Jim, Jack, and the cowpunchers had made their last stand. Jim was never so glad to see anyone in his life!

The cook moved the chuck wagon back to the fire and resumed cooking, and the cowboys went looking for the scattered horses. They had to recover the horse cavvy before they did anything else

CHAPTER 23

Ben and Jill

When the 4-C crew reached the place where Ben remembered Jill trading them five apple pies for a couple of wagonloads of baby calves, Ben Walker bid the rest of crew goodbye and decided he'd try and find out where Jill lived.

"So that's why you've been looking like a lost calf on the drive down?" jived Jack.

"You're just jealous" was Ben's return as he turned his horse off the trail. Of course the wagon tracks left by her wagon when she met with the herd two months previously would have been wiped out with wind and rain. But Ben had seen the direction from which the wagon approached when she drove up to their camp that morning, so he rode in that direction. He looked for any sign of what might be smoke rising from a chimney.

He came to a creek and stopped. He was in need of a bath. So he dismounted and tied his horse to a tree limb. He reached into his saddlebags and found a clean shirt and some clean pants. He also pulled out a sliver of soap. He pulled off his clothes and waded down into the icy stream. After his bath, he put his clean clothes on and put his dirty clothes back into his saddlebags. Then he started a fire. He heated water to shave. He got a hand mirror out of his saddlebag and placed it into the fork of a tree limb and got out his shaving soap, brush, and razor. He undid his belt and pulled the end of it out so he could strop his razor. Then he refastened his belt and started shaving.

After he bathed and shaved and got his six-gun in place, he remounted his horse and continued his search for Jill's cabin. He finally saw a plume of smoke rising as if from a campfire or chimney and turned his horse toward it. Before he saw the cabin, he saw a pasture made from a rail fence with goats grazing inside. And he saw some calves that looked to be a couple of months old out scampering around. Some of them were nursing the nanny goats. Then he saw the cabin and rode over in that direction. It was nearly noon, so she'd probably be cooking dinner.

He rode up to the cabin and called out, "Hello, the house!"

Jill opened the door a crack and stuck her head out. "Who is it?" she asked.

"It's Ben," he answered. Then she recognized his face.

"Why, hello. Put your horse in the corral and unsaddle him. You're just in time for dinner."

Ben saw little Jacob's head peeking around the door facing behind Jill. Jill closed the door. After he unsaddled his horse and closed the corral gate, he came back to the cabin. She told him to sit down at the table. Little Jacob hid behind his mother's skirt. Then Jill started putting food on the table. Since he was holding on to her skirt, she pulled him back and forth with her from the stove to the kitchen table.

Supper turned out to be a goat pot roast with beans, biscuits, and gravy. She took the coffeepot off the fire and poured him a cup of coffee. Then she poured a cup for herself. She poured a glass of goat's milk for Jacob, and they started eating. The food was delicious. It was the first time Ben had eaten a woman's cooking in years. Jill noticed how handsome he looked. He was clean-shaven and his hair was combed neat. And she also felt a certain warmth inside her little cabin that wasn't there before.

"So you and Jacob just live here all alone?" Ben asked.

"Yes," she replied. For some reason, she felt like talking.

"My husband was killed at Gettysburg four years ago. Hank homesteaded this farm and had proved it up before the war started. Then he went off to war. I never saw him again." She wiped a tear out of the corner of her eye.

"But we made a home of this place. Hank had been raising corn and hogs, but when he left, I sold all the hogs. And I couldn't manage a walking plow pulled by a horse, so I traded some of the hogs for dairy goats before I sold all of them. I milked them at first and took butter and cream into town to sell. And I kept all our chickens and had eggs to sell every week or so. We had a granary full of corn to feed them.

"But when the nanny goats had kids, I kept all the female ones and made milk goats out of them too. It got so it was too much of a chore to milk them all. But I found a calf beside a dead cow on the way to town one day and lifted it into the wagon and brought it home. I go to town about twice a week to sell eggs. And I go to church every Sunday.

"I decided to see if I could get the calf to nurse one of the goats. I tied the goat to the corral fence and tied the goat's hind feet together. This way, the calf could suck without being kicked away. Then trail drives started going by, and I found out they shot any baby calves that were born during the drive. So I started going out in my wagon and getting baby calves from them. I can barely live on the eggs I sell, but when the calves get up to weaning size, I can sell them to ranchers."

Ben just listened to her. He didn't ask any questions. He'd nod his head occasionally, and sometimes, he'd make some reply such as "Really!" but mostly, he just listened. She explained that she didn't meet very many cowboys because cowboys normally didn't go to church, and besides, cowboys didn't really go to town to get supplies very often if they were working for a ranch. The cook or cook's helper normally went in to buy supplies. That answered a question for Ben that he didn't have to ask. He figured as pretty as she was, she'd be flooded with cowboy suitors.

After dinner, she heated some water on the stove to wash the dishes. She continued telling him her life's story while she did the dishes. After she was done, she asked him if he'd like to go see her goats and calves.

He said, "Yes, I'd like to do that."

"Can I come?" Jacob asked.

"Yes, but mind your manners and don't interrupt Mr. Walker while he's talking," she replied.

As they left the cabin, he noticed she was wearing a dress that was old and faded and tattered in places. And he noticed a pair of man's work shoes just below the hem of her dress. Her hair had been combed neatly and was fastened in a bun on the back of her head. She had no makeup on her face nor did she wear any jewelry. And he thought she was beautiful.

Little Jacob was barefoot and wearing patched overalls. He scampered around and started telling Ben about how the calves liked to play.

She led Ben to a gate in the rail fence. He hurried ahead to open it for her. She walked through the gate, and he followed, closing and fastening the gate after her. She was still in the mood to talk. She walked around the pasture talking about the mama goats and how she had trained them to let the calves nurse.

"I had to tie the nanny's head to a fence post and tie her hind legs. But she'd fight it every time just doing it that way. I found if I took the baby calf and held it up to her nose and made her smell it, she'd still fight it, but after that, she'd calm down a bit. Then I'd hold the calf's nose up to her and make her smell its breath. Then I'd give her a minute or two to get used to it, then I'd hold the calf's head to her udder until it started nursing. It seems that after she got used to the smell of the calf, she started thinking it was her own baby and she'd let it nurse. So after that, I didn't have to tie her legs anymore. Or her head. I had to do that for every nanny in the herd. But I got all the calves to nursing. The calves all think the nanny goats are their mothers, and the nanny goats all think the calves are their own offspring now."

"What happened to the nanny's kids?" was a question that Ben thought of.

"I sold them to a restaurant in town" was her answer. "I didn't get much for them, but when they get grown, they still aren't worth much. Cattle bring a much better price. The calves will nurse the nanny goats until they're weaning size. Then I'll turn them into a bigger pasture, where they'll finish growing up on grass. In a few years, they'll be big enough to sell to someone starting a trail herd to take to Kansas."

They continued to wander around the pasture, and Jill told Ben the name of each nanny goat they came to—except when Jacob quipped up before she got a chance. He knew all the names of the mama goats too. And each calf also had a name. It was obvious to Ben that she really enjoyed caring for livestock, but her idea of using dairy goats to raise baby calves was a very novel idea to him. And while little Jacob was too small to be much help, it looked like he must have been out trying to help her whenever he could. They came to a creek in a corner of the pasture where the goats would go to water. She sat down on a big rock that had room for Ben and Jacob to sit beside her. Ben sat down too.

"You haven't told me anything about yourself," Jill remarked.

"I'd rather learn about you," was his answer.

"I've been telling you about me," she said in turn.

"Yes, and it is all very interesting," he said.

"But I want to know about you," she insisted.

"There isn't much to tell," he said.

"Where are you from?" she asked.

"I was born in Tennessee and grew up there."

"Were you a farm boy?" she asked.

"Not exactly. We raised Thoroughbred horses. Then along came the war, and I joined up with a cavalry regiment. I went all through the war and then came to Texas to be a cowboy. Since all I knew was horses, it seemed like the only kind of job I could get doing what I wanted to do."

"So you mainly like horses?" she queried.

"Yes, but I like cattle too. I didn't really know that much about cattle till I started cowboying. I mainly like the wide, open spaces and working on horseback. It seems to be something I'm good at. I can ride any bronc no matter how rough, and I'm good with a rope."

So it was his turn to talk. She became the listener. They continued to talk until the sun started getting low enough in the sky that she said, "Will you stay for supper?"

He said sure.

Little Jacob immediately popped up with, "Can I set by you while we eat?"

"Mind your manners, Jacob," Jill reminded him.

"Okay," he said meekly. He obviously was a boy that wanted to please his mother. He just got carried away easily as seemed to be the case with all five-year-olds.

So they headed back toward the cabin. After supper, Ben made his leave. He thought it would be important to leave at a respectable hour.

"Can't Ben stay all night?" asked Jake?

"Jake, mind your manners," his mother admonished him again.

After Ben walked out and saddled his horse to ride off, she went out into the yard to say goodbye to him. It was already dark by then. When he rode off into the darkness, she suddenly started feeling very, very lonely.

"Will he come back?" Jacob wanted to know.

"I hope so," she replied.

Ben rode just a little way until he found a place to camp. He was overcome with loneliness too.

Vickie Again

When the 4-C crew arrived back in Texas, Jim headed straight for Waco of course. It was a Sunday afternoon, so he rode to the Allen residence. He rode around to the back and put his horse in the stable as if he owned the place. The Allen residence did feel like home to him. He unsaddled his horse, took the bridle and saddle to the tack room, and took off his chaps and spurs before he left the stable and started back toward the house. Walking past the backyard, he saw Vickie sitting in a lawn chair. She was holding a puppy in her lap and was stroking it and talking baby talk to it. Of course, the puppy was enjoying all the attention it was getting. It was a little collie puppy. And Vickie was preoccupied with her new pet and hadn't noticed Jim riding to the stable and wasn't aware of him now standing, looking at her from over the backyard fence. It was a white picket fence, which was common in the finer homes of the day.

It wasn't until Jim moved to walk over to the gate that Vickie looked up and saw him. She squealed with delight and set the puppy down and ran to meet him just as he walked into the yard. He had to brace himself to keep from being knocked down when she reached him and grabbed him around the neck. He lifted her and spun her around twice like always before he put her feet back on the ground and reached down to give her a kiss. Then she clung to him as if for dear life for several minutes before she let go. The poor abandoned puppy looked up at them as if to say, Who is this interloper? All her attention was on Jim now.

Then Jim looked over Vickie's head at the little puppy and said, "Who is your new friend?"

Vickie turned her head to glance over her shoulder and said, "Oh, that's Scamp. My new puppy." And she turned and reached down and picked him up to show him to Jim. She handed him to Jim, and he immediately licked Jim in the face. Jim sat down in the lawn chair, placed the puppy in his lap, and stroked it.

"It is a cute puppy," Jim said.

"Why don't you teach him some tricks while I go in and help Mama cook supper?" she asked and got up.

"Okay," Jim said as she walked into the house.

Now Jim did have some experience training puppies, though he didn't see how Vickie could know about it. They kept fox hounds on the plantation he grew up on. One of the dogs would have a litter occasionally and he and his father would train them to be hunting dogs as soon as they were big enough.

So he placed the puppy on the ground and said, "Sit." The puppy looked at him, making it clear he had no idea what he meant. Jim put his hand on the puppy's little rump and pushed it to the ground forcing him to sit. Then he told him what a smart little puppy he was like as if he had done it on his own.

Then he said, "Up," and took hold of the puppy's rump with both hands and pulled him back to a standing position.

After alternating between those two commands and putting the puppy in position by hand with each command, he had the puppy sitting and standing on command in just a few minutes.

When Vickie came back outside several minutes later, Jim showed her how her puppy would sit and stand on command. She was amazed.

"You taught him all of that just in a couple of minutes!" she exclaimed.

"Yes," Jim said. "He's a smart puppy." Then he said, "You try it."

So Vickie said, "Sit." The little puppy's rump hit the grass.

Then Jim said, "Now brag on him."

So Vickie said, "Nice puppy," in a very affectionate tone of voice. The little feller wagged his tail and wiggled in appreciation of her praise.

Then she said, "Up," and he stood up again. She told him what a nice puppy he was again.

"That is neat," she said. "So you *can* train a puppy. How do I teach him to come when I call him?"

Jim explained that he had learned all they should expect him to for a first lesson. "Just have him practice what he has just now learned for the next few days. Then teach him to stay. Then after another few days, have him stay, walk off a few steps and tell him to come. Then go over and pull him up and walk him to where she was standing when she said "Come. And to keep doing that until he understands what you mean by that command."

Vickie was even more excited about her new puppy now that she had some idea about how to train him. Jim knew he could train him to be a cow dog after he got big enough.

"Can you stay this time and finish training my puppy?" she asked.

Jim explained how he still needed to go find a place to start a ranch and that he already had a herd of five hundred young cows and twenty young bulls wearing his brand.

"But I still need to find a place to file for a homestead and build a barn, corral, and ranch house and all. And I need to make another trip to West Texas and catch some more horses." Vickie's feathers fell when she heard that. It meant he'd be leaving again.

Then Jim reached into his pocket and pulled out a small box. He opened the box and showed her a set of rings. He put one ring on her finger. It was an engagement ring. He showed her the other ring. It was a wedding ring.

"I'm asking you to set us a wedding date for this fall," he said. "In November."

"I have to wait until November?" she replied.

"It's nearly July now," he answered. "We need to wait a respectable amount of time before we have the ceremony," he said.

"But you're ready to set the date!" What he was communicating finally reached her. "We can finally get married!" She was elated. She stood up and grabbed him and got him in a bear hug. He barely had time to get to his feet before her arms were around him. She clung to him for several minutes.

Then Vickie told him they'd wait until her father came home from work and then announce their engagement to her father and mother both at the same time over supper.

Then Vickie told Jim she wanted him to come in and play music while waiting for supper to cook. So they left the puppy in the backyard and went inside. The puppy whined and carried on at first, but Vickie opened the back door and gave him a bone to chew on, so after a few minutes, he occupied himself with that and permitted the two humans to leave him alone in the backyard.

Jim and Vickie went inside, and Jim greeted Vickie's mother. She had flour on her hands and arms and couldn't hug him, but she leaned toward him so he could hug her.

Then Vickie brought Jim his mandolin and sat down at the piano, and Jim tuned his mandolin. They had time to play a few songs and get warmed up before her father came home from work.

The next morning, Jim, over breakfast, said to Vickie, "I need to go and buy a chuck wagon and start hiring a crew."

"Why do you need to leave so soon?" she asked him.

He said, "I don't have to leave yet. It will take several days to get ready. But I need more horses, and I need more cattle if I'm going to start a ranch."

"It's so good to have you home again," she told him.

"It's good to be home again." The Allens' house did seem more like home to Jim than any other place he'd been since he'd left South Carolina four years previously.

"So you're going to be gone all day?" Vickie asked.

"Yes."

"Then I'll go help Papa at the store. He needs help but doesn't want to hire anyone if he can help it. He likes having me help him because I know the store. If he hired someone, he'd have to train them."

"But you'll be home again tonight?"

"Yep, I should be home by suppertime," Jim answered.

CHAPTER 25

Getting His Own Crew Together

Jim headed his horse to the place where the chuck wagon was camped. They had camped west of town about ten miles or so. He saw the horse cavvy first then saw the white canvas of the chuck wagon. He rode up to the fire. Ben and several cowboys were sitting at the fire having coffee. The horse wrangler was out watching the horses. Jim dismounted, got a cup of coffee, and then asked Ben, "Where is Jack?"

"He's in town. He's taken a shine to a waitress that works at the restaurant there," Ben told him.

"Do you know when he'll be back?" Jim asked.

"Hopefully this afternoon. He planned to buy some supplies and ride on back. But I'll bet he stopped by the restaurant for coffee."

It was midmorning. So Jim decided to ride back to town and try to find Jack. He rode up to the restaurant, and sure enough, he saw Jack's horse tied to the hitch rail. He dismounted, tied his own mount to the rail, and went in.

He walked in and saw Jack sitting at a table with this beautiful girl filling up his coffee cup. She had on a light-blue dress trimmed in white and had her hair done up on top of her head. Jim walked up and sat down in the chair across from Jack.

"Why, hello," Jack said. "This is Jeannie. Jeannie, this is Jim."

"Why, I remember you," Jim said. "Saw you at a dance once."

"Yes! I remember you too!" Then after a pause, she asked, "Do you want coffee?"

"Yep," Jim answered.

"Cream and sugar?"

"Nope, just black."

"She's a beautiful girl," Jim remarked.

"Yeah. A war window," Jack returned.

"Well, she seems to be a really fine lady."

"Yep, she's that."

Jim had met Jeannie shortly after he arrived in Waco. She seemed to take a shine to him; but his thoughts were all on Vickie, so he didn't notice it when she made eyes at him.

"I decided I'd drop by and talk about what we'll do next," Jim then said to Jack.

"I need to just go back to my ranch and get some branding caught up," Jack said. "We did no branding at all during the war."

"Well, I'm thinking about going after some more mustangs. I still need more horses."

"You can do that. You probably should just buy yourself a chuck wagon now so you'll have it. I don't think the cowboys will all want to go join my branding crew. Some of them might want to ride with you."

So Jim decided he'd figure out which men wanted to stay with Jack or if any of them wanted to join up with him.

Jim rode back to the chuck wagon and talked to the men there. Ben was still at the fire. "Anyone want to go wild horse hunting?" Jim asked.

"I'll go with you," Ben said. "I'd like to catch some mustangs."

It turned out that four more of the men wanted to join Jim's mustanging crew. The other five decided to join Jack's branding crew. The men that joined Jim's crew in addition to Ben were Jeb, Gene, Gil, and Russ.

"I'm going to buy a chuck wagon and team," Jim told them. "Where will you be?"

"At the saloon," Jeb said.

"Yeah, me too," Gene answered. Gil and Russ said the same.

"You can just wait for me at the saloon then," Jim said. "It will probably be midafternoon or so. I'm planning to camp over about a mile from here. It'll still be near the creek. Ben, could you cut out my horses and take them down there before you leave for town?"

"I don't plan to go to town," Ben answered. "I'll just take your horses down there, make camp, and wait for you."

So Jim mounted his horse and headed for town again. He found a place in Waco that sold horses and chuck wagons and such. He walked up to a man who looked like a storekeeper. He shook hands with him and introduced himself, then said, "I need a chuck wagon and two teams of horses to pull it." You only needed one team to pull a chuck wagon, but he wanted to swap teams each day so the horses could rest some every other day.

There was a long line of wagons to look at. Jim walked down and just took a cursory look at each one first. A kinda off-white canvas covered each wagon, but Jim looked at the hitch and the wagon tongue of each to make sure they were in good shape.

"I'd like to hitch a team to one of them and try it out first," Jim then said.

"I have a pen of horses right over there. You could buy the horses first then decide which wagon to try out," the trader told him.

Jim and the trader walked over to the horse pen, and Jim picked out four good work horses. He took two of them over to the wagon he had chosen and hitched them up. Then the trader opened the gate, let him drive through, closed it, and got up into the seat beside him. Jim figured the only way to find out if the axles were sound was to see how it rode. He drove down the road apiece then came back.

After some brief bickering, they closed the deal, and Jim paid him with gold and silver coins. He tied the spare team and his saddle horse behind the wagon and drove off. He stopped at the Allen store first to buy some supplies. They'd need things to cook for the crew. Vickie waited on him, and he paid her. Then he went out, got in the chuck wagon, and drove it toward the place where he had instructed Ben to camp with his horse herd.

When he drove up to the camp, he saw Ben. He was loose herding the horses. Ben rode over toward him with his hand near his gun. Then he recognized Jim.

"Looks like we have a chuck wagon now," Ben remarked.

"Yep, now I need to hire some cowboys."

Ben dismounted to help Jim unhitch the team. He took all the new wagon horses and turned them loose in the horse herd. Then he walked to the fire and poured a cup of coffee. Ben had agreed to stay in camp and watch the horses, but he apparently kept a pot of coffee going. Jim rolled a smoke, then sipped his coffee and puffed his cigarette.

"Everything going okay here?" Jim asked.

"Pretty quiet," Ben answered.

It was close enough to noon that Jim decided to stay and help Ben cook dinner and then eat before riding off again. After they'd eaten, Jim mounted his horse and headed back to town.

Jim rode up to the saloon. He tied his horse to the hitch rail and walked around to the boardwalk. He stopped and pushed the swinging doors open. He saw several gamblers already at the card games. He walked to the bar and asked the bartender, "Have you seen any out of work cowboys around here?"

"I saw three yesterday. They're camped out south of town. They said they're about five miles out."

"Thanks," Jim said and walked back out.

He mounted and rode to their camp. They were sitting by their campfire drinking coffee. Their hobbled horses were grazing nearby.

"Hello, the fire," Jim said as he rode up. "I'm riding friendly."

"Git down and have some coffee," one of them told him.

Jim dismounted, tied his horse to a tree, and walked to the fire. One of the men handed him a steel cup, and he filled it with coffee from the coffeepot.

"I'm looking for out-of-work cowboys," he told them.

"All three of us are looking for work." the same puncher told him.

"I'm Jim Bennett. Just got back from a drive to Abilene," Jim then said.

"I'm Waylon. This is Pete"—he gestured to a cowboy sitting on a log and sipping coffee—"and that's Matt." Matt was sitting on a big rock sipping coffee also.

"I'm looking for hands to go mustanging. It will be in Indian country, so you'll need to keep your rifles handy. I also plan to chase up some wild cattle after that. We'll trail break them and take them to Abilene."

"When do we start?" asked Waylon.

"You can break camp, saddle up, and ride with me to the chuck wagon now" was Jim's answer. "You'll get thirty a month, grub, and a place to unroll your bedroll near the chuck wagon."

So the men put out the fire, caught up their horses, and saddled them. They rode off with Jim.

He and Jack had split up the horses upon their return to Texas, so he already had twenty-five horses. But Jim decided he'd better buy some more riding stock. He rode back to town and stopped at a horse trader's corral. He found fifteen horses that looked like they'd make good saddle horses. He'd find more later. Besides, they'd get some more horses to rough break after they'd caught some mustangs.

It was nearly suppertime by then so he rode back over to the Allen place. He put his horse in the stable and walked around to the house. He went in. Vickie and her ma were already cooking supper.

"Can we play music tonight?" Vickie asked him.

"Sure," answered Jim.

"How did your day go?" Vickie then asked.

"Pretty good. I bought a chuck wagon and team and hired three cowboys today. I also bought some more saddle horses. I still need a cook."

After supper, Vickie sat down at the piano, and Jim tuned up his mandolin. They played music for several hours.

CHAPTER 26

Jim Hires a New Horse Wrangler

The next morning, Jim saddled up Buck and rode over to the General Store.

"I need to hire a cook," he told the storekeeper. "Do you know anyone who can cook that needs a job?"

"Actually, I do. He's a cowboy who broke his leg last year and, after it healed up, decided to quit cowboying. He's made a trip to Abilene already as a chuck wagon cook. He's a good cook. He came in a few days ago to see if I knew of any place he could find a job."

"Where can I find him?"

"He's living in a cabin on the south side of town. He's married and is living there with his wife."

Jim got directions to his place and rode on over. He found him sitting on the front porch whittling on a piece of wood.

He looked up at Jim. "Get down and sit awhile," he said. Jim found out his name was Charlie.

"I need a chuck wagon cook. I'm going West to Indian country to catch some wild mustangs. Then I'm going to build up a herd of wild cattle and take them to Abilene."

"I need a job," Charlie responded. "When do we start?"

"In a couple of days."

"Let me go tell Emma. Emma, can you come out here a minute?" he yelled.

A middle-aged woman came to the door. "Meet my new boss. We're going to take a herd up the trail so I have a job now. His name is Jim."

Jim told Charlie that if he'd be ready the following morning, he'd take him out to the chuck wagon.

Jim then rode back to the chuck wagon and got there at about noon. He dismounted, loosened the cinch on his saddle, and tied his horse to one of the wagon wheels.

Ben and the three new cowboys were there. They were cooking dinner.

"I hired us a new cook," he told them. "He starts tomorrow."

"I'm glad of that," said Waylon. "I don't like having to eat my own cooking."

The other four cowboys that had come down with them from Abilene were to meet them before they left town to head west.

Jim rode over to the Allen house again. Vickie and Mr. Allen were still at work, but he greeted Mrs. Allen and told her he was going to work with the pup some in the backyard. Scamp wagged his tail as soon as he saw him and acted like he was an old friend he hadn't seen in ages. Jim reviewed with him all he had taught him so far. It apparently made the pup's day to get another training session.

*****

After five days, it came time for Jim to saddle up and ride off with his crew. He needed to find a place to establish the homestead itself, but he figured he needed more horses and more cattle too. So eight cowboys and Jim rode off with the cook driving the chuck wagon and headed southwest. He still needed to hire a horse wrangler and a cook's helper. He figured he'd find them and more cowboys as they rode along.

The weather was hot as they rode along to the southwest through the Texas brush country. As they rode, they saw a thin plume of smoke several miles ahead almost in their path of travel. Jim told Ben to take the horse herd over to the right to ride around the smoke.

He rode to each man individually and gave each one this message: "I'm leaving Ben in charge as the ramrod. I'm going to investigate that smoke." He pointed toward it. Then he spurred his buckskin on ahead until he was out of sight of the Slant JB crew.

He paused periodically to look for tracks to give him some idea of what might have happened. He did see some unshod horse tracks. He walked his horse along and also saw some boot tracks. So someone walked by here too, but not an Indian. And the tracks were small enough he could tell they weren't from a man full grown. Then he urged his horse forward, looking each direction cautiously.

When he got close, he stopped and rode a careful circle around the spot where the smoke seemed to come from. He learned quickly that it was the smoking ruins of a farmhouse and barn—Indians. He didn't think they were in Indian country yet. The Indians must have made a raid out of their territory.

As he rode closer, he saw what looked like a boy in his midteens with a shovel. As he rode still closer, he saw two graves, and the boy was shoveling dirt over one of them. The other grave had already been filled in. As he rode on up, he saw the boy put down the shovel, and he started fashioning a cross out of two sticks of wood. He tied them together with rawhide. He then took the butt end of a hatchet and drove the cross into the ground at the head of one of the graves. The boy looked up and immediately dropped his hatchet and ran over to a nearby tree when he saw Jim. He grabbed a rifle that was leaning against it and leveled it at Jim. Jim didn't move. He just sat his horse. After a few seconds, the boy figured out that Jim wasn't a threat and lowered his rifle.

"My parents were killed by Indians," he sobbed. Jim could see the tears streaming down his face. He didn't look like more than thirteen or fourteen years old.

Jim dismounted. He led the buckskin to the tree where the boy had retrieved his rifle when he first saw Jim and tied him to it. "Let's put an epitaph on the markers," was all Jim said.

He went over to the woodpile where there was still a rick of wood and picked out a couple of pieces. He motioned to the boy to loan him his hatchet. He split the wood into thirds. The middle piece made a pretty decent plank about three feet long. He did the same with another piece of wood. Then he borrowed the boy's shovel and moved around some of the still-burning coals of what was left of the toolshed into a pile so it made a fire of its own. He put the hatchet blade in the edge of the fire. After it was hot, he etched into the plank, "Here Lies…" and then asked the boy his father's name.

"Henry Allstat," the boy answered.

After he had finished burning the epitaph for his father, he did a similar one for his mother's grave marker.

"And your mother's name?"

"Molly." The boy's tears had dried by now.

After he finished the epitaph for the mom, he took the hatchet and drove the markers into the ground at the head of each grave.

"What's your name?" he asked.

"Mark," the boy said.

"Jim," Jim replied and held out his hand. The boy took it and shook hands with him. "Any relatives near here?" Jim asked.

"No," the boy replied. "I have no one now."

"Want a job?" Jim asked.

The boy looked up at Jim. "You have a job for me?"

"I need a horse wrangler."

"But I have no horse or anything. The Indians stole our two plow horses, our milk cow, burned the chicken house, and killed the chickens and stole our two hogs. They killed the hogs and put them on one of their horses and took them with them."

"I have horses for you to ride," Jim explained.

So Jim had the boy get up on his horse behind him, and they started riding back toward his crew. The boy insisted on bringing his rifle. It was actually his father's rifle, but the Indians didn't get it because he was out hunting for meat when they came. It was a .54-caliber Hawkins muzzleloader. Jim knew that the Hawkins was an accurate shooting gun. Mark picked up the powder horn off the ground and put it on his shoulder just before he mounted up. He already had a bullet pouch at this belt.

"I planned to bring back some venison," he explained. The sobbing was out of his voice by now.

So Jim took his new horse wrangler back to the Slant JB chuck wagon and introduced him to the crew. It was nearly noon, so they halted to rest the horses and cook their noon meal.

When they roped a horse each after they broke camp, Jim roped a bay gelding and saddled it for Mark. He had several spare saddles in the chuck wagon and bridles too. Then he explained, "This will be your horse for today. Your job will be to just ride alongside the horses for now. When we get started running cattle, you'll move the horses up for each cowboy to get a fresh horse when he needs it."

Jim also brought a saddle boot from the chuck wagon and fastened it to his saddle. "Here is a place to put your rifle," he said.

So Mark placed his rifle in the saddle boot and mounted up.

Jim Hires an Indian

They continued their ride toward mustang country. Jim made the practice of either himself or Ben scouting ahead each day to make sure there would be no surprises on the trail. One morning, while Jim was taking his turn as scout, he started up a rise and smelled a familiar smell—the smell of dead bodies. He continued very cautiously on up the rise only to find the scene of a fight between two Indian tribes. It appeared that a Comanche war party had met up with an Apache party and that the Comanches had lost. Jim found four dead Comanches and a fifth one tied between two trees with rawhide thongs fastened to his wrists. Jim couldn't tell if he was alive or not. He rode around the area several times to make sure there were no hostiles still around before he approached the brave and dismounted. The brave's head was dangling down toward his chest and he was hanging from the rawhide thongs holding him between the two trees. His hands were purple. Jim touched the body and it was still warm. He'd be cold by now if he was dead. Jim took out his hunting knife and very carefully cut him loose. He grabbed him and held him while he cut each thong. After he cut the second thong, he eased him to the ground. Then he did the more delicate task of cutting the tightened rawhide from the Indian's wrists.

The Indian roused up then, so Jim went and got his canteen from his saddle and came back to offer the Indian a drink. The Indian raised his head up but didn't take hold of the canteen. Jim figured out that he couldn't move his hands, so he held the canteen to his mouth so he could drink. Jim put the canteen up to his lips and poured a swallow of water into his mouth. The Indian swallowed it eagerly then started coughing. After his fit of coughing subsided, Jim started massaging his hands. They were cold as ice and still blue. And his wrists had blood on them where the wet rawhide had cut into his skin as it dried and tightened.

After a few minutes, Jim gave him another swallow of water and then massaged his hands some more. The Indian opened his eyes then and looked at him, wondering who would help a dying Indian. But Jim noticed that his hands were starting to return to their natural color. He gave him another sip of water.

After thirty minutes or so, Jim's canteen was empty, and the Indian was able to use his hands. Jim went to his saddlebags and got some bandages to bandage his wrists. He asked the Indian if he could stand. But then, he probably didn't speak English. The Indian said yes and got up but with difficulty. He was obviously still weak. But Jim learned that he did speak English after all!

So Jim mounted and started to help him up behind his saddle, but the Indian pulled away, walked a few steps, and picked up a bow and a quiver of arrows from the ground. The Apaches, in their haste, had left them. He put the quiver of arrows and the bow on his back and then mounted up behind Jim.

Jim had crossed a creek a few miles back. He rode back to the creek, dismounted, and helped the Indian down so he could finish drinking his fill of water from the creek. Jim refilled his canteen.

Then they remounted. The Indian was much stronger after getting his fill of water. Jim rode on back to the chuck wagon and horse herd. It was noon by now, and the chuck wagon had halted. The cook was cooking the noon meal.

Jim helped the Indian down and poured a cup of hot coffee from the coffeepot and handed it to him. Then he poured another for himself.

After the Indian had several sips of hot coffee, he asked him his name.

"I am He Who Flies," the Indian answered.

Then Jim said, "Can you tell me what happened?"

"Comanches were looking for wild horses. We knew we'd have to come further south than usual to find them." Jim noticed he spoke English very fluently. And he was curious about that but didn't interrupt.

"The Apache claim this land as their own, so they attacked us for being on their land. The Apache claims all the land in this area and all the wild horses to be Apache property. So they attacked us without warning. Of twelve of us, four were killed and scalped, and I was knocked unconscious by a blow from a tomahawk. Since I was captured alive, they tied me up as you saw me. The last I saw were the rest of my party in a running battle with the Apaches. I do not know what happened to them. The two that tied me up rode after them."

Then Jim noticed a cut in the Indian's scalp. But it was clotted over with blood, so he decided it was okay without a bandage. It would be a hard place to put a bandage anyway.

When Cookie had the meal ready, Jim prepared a plate for He Who Flies and handed it to him. He started eating with his fingers before Jim could hand him a fork. But he accepted the fork and then started eating with it.

When four of the cowboys rode up and dismounted to eat, two of them, Jeb and Gene, saw the Indian, and Jeb pulled out his gun as if to shoot him. Jim struck his hand and made him drop his gun.

"I'm not going to eat at the same fire as an Indian!" he protested.

"You don't have to eat if you don't want to," Jim retorted. Gene hadn't gone for his gun, but he pulled his arm back as if to backhand the Indian across the mouth. Jim blocked his blow and hit him two really hard blows in the gut then another on the jaw, knocking him down.

"Both of you are fired," Jim then told them. "You can still have grub first if you like, but then you'll saddle up your personal horses and ride out." He stepped back and held his hand near his gun in case they wanted to make their argument more physical.

Both of them did get a plate of grub and walked off about fifty feet from the fire to eat. Jim stood watching them with his hand near his gun. Then when Mark came up, he told him to go rope their personal horses one at a time and bring them to the fire. He described the horses that belonged to them.

When they had finished eating, Jim said, "Get your pay from the cook."

Charlie got the money bag out of his grub box where he kept it and counted out their pay. Jim kept his hand near his gun all that time. Jim didn't eat until both of them had finished with their grub, saddled up their personal mounts, and then ridden off.

He Who Flies was on his third helping by then. Jim finally got a plate of grub, sat down next to He Who Flies and said, "You can camp with us until your wrists are healed and you feel like traveling. And you can stay longer than that if you like." Jim then asked, "And why do you speak such good English?" He finally got the time to satisfy his curiosity in that regard.

"I was adopted by missionaries when I was a boy. My parents were killed in a fight with white men when I was six years old. I went to school at a mission until I was ten. Then the mission was attacked and all the priests and nuns were killed and I lived with Comanches again until I was grown."

Well, that explained why he spoke such good English.

*****

As they rode toward mustang country, Jim continued with his routine scouts of the country ahead so he could avoid any surprises he could prevent. They were clear of the brush country now and into just rolling prairies though they still had small mesquite bushes interspersed with the soapweed. But there was lots of grass too. There was still plenty of forage for the horses to graze, and for the buffalo and wild cattle, too, for that matter. Jim decided to scout their back trail just to make sure no one was following them. He didn't think Jeb and Gene would be content just to ride off.

He had started the habit of making his first scout early in the morning before the cook even got up to start breakfast. This morning, when he put on his hat and pulled on his boots, it was still dark. Since he kept a horse tied to the wagon wheel, he didn't have to worry about roping a horse. He was riding his buckskin this morning. He was still his favorite horse.

Jim decided to ride back and check their back trail that morning first, before breakfast. At first light, he saw a plume of smoke about ten miles behind their camp. He kept riding until he got close to the smoke. Then he rode on up slowly and dismounted behind several boulders. He tied the buckskin to a bush and climbed up slowly. He could just see their camp. He recognized Jeb and Gene cooking breakfast over their fire. So! Jeb and Gene were following them!

There was no law against them camping where they were. But Jim decided he'd better continue to keep his eye on their back trail just in case.

The following morning, he went to check their back trail again and saw Jeb and Gene's camp again. This wasn't good. It *did* appear they were following them. But the third morning, they were gone. So Jim concluded that they had decided to finally ride on off. The more problems they could anticipate beforehand, the easier it would be to handle them; but maybe this was a problem that wasn't going to materialize after all.

Mark bunched up the horses and got them started toward the chuck wagon. It was nearly noon, and he wanted to make sure he had the horses at the chuck wagon in time for the cowboys to change mounts. It was his first job other than working for his father on their farm.

He was still somewhat in a state of grief at the loss of his parents. He was at the point where he didn't know what he was going to do. But hard work is a therapy that helps make emotional wounds heal. And he was accustomed to work. Things like following a walking plow or hoeing corn were things he had plenty of experience doing. Riding a horse all day was something he wasn't used to. He was sore all over. But the physical soreness just helped draw his attention away from his recent loss, so his spirits were actually higher because of it.

He brought the horses in, and the cook, the cook's flunky, and Mark made their rope triangle to run them into so the boys could rope a fresh mount after they ate. So after he finished eating, Jim untied the horse he had tied to the wagon wheel, led him into the rope triangle, took off his saddle and bridle, and turned him loose. Then he roped a fresh horse, put the bridle on him, and saddled him. He had chosen a gray horse this time. He spurred the gray into a gallop to move up to the head of the horse herd. The cowboys all rode around the horses and kept them bunched up until the cook, the cook's helper, and Mark finished eating.

Jim and Ben still wanted to keep up their scouting ahead of their path of travel. But Jim continued to spend some time scouting their back trail as well. Ben wanted to go with him. He didn't see any harm in that, so he let Ben come along.

Ben liked the new outfit. He liked being in Jim's crew. He just felt like Jim was probably the best boss he had ever had. But his thoughts ranged to Jill and little Jacob pretty often as he rode, especially since they didn't have much to do. Jacob was such a cute little fella. And Jill was such a beautiful woman. And he still thought it was neat about her using nanny goats to raise calves when he thought about it again. Now a cowboy would be laughed off the range if he was caught raising goats. But a woman could get away with it.

After riding about ten miles or so behind their line of travel, they still didn't see any evidence of being followed, so they turned back toward the path the chuck wagon had taken. They'd catch up with them by supper time with no problem.

At camp that night, Jim got out his harmonica. And they found out that Ben had brought a guitar. He normally kept it in the chuck wagon. So he tuned up his guitar and played along with Jim. Cowboys do have to sing even if they sound like a coyote with a sore toe. They had to sing to the cattle while on night guard to keep them from getting spooked by the sound of a saddle squeaking. But Jim had a good singing voice, and it turned out that Ben did too. So they sang and played until they were tired. Then they turned in.

CHAPTER 28

The Allen Family Goes to Church

It was Sunday morning, and the Allen family was all dressed up and had climbed into their carriage to go to church. There was room for all three to sit in the seat of the carriage. Mr. Allen popped his whip over the bay mare, and she started off at a snappy trot.

The Allen family did not go to church every Sunday. If there were trail drives near Waco, Mr. Allen kept his store open seven days a week. The cowboys normally didn't know what day of the week it was. Some of them didn't even know the month. Calendars were unheard of at chuck wagons. They just knew it was summertime.

But this morning, there were no trail drives near Waco, so Mr. Allen closed his store and took his family to church.

The Allen residence was in the southern part of town, and the church building was on the northern side. When they arrived, Mr. Allen maneuvered the carriage alongside the last carriage that was parked in a line of carriages. Then he got out and tied the reins to the long hitching post that ran along the end of the churchyard. Then he walked around and helped Mrs. Allen out of the carriage. Then he put up a hand for Vickie to help her out of the carriage too. Vickie was wearing a light-blue dress with ruffles and a light-blue cap to match. She looked really pretty. Louise Allen was wearing a light-green dress also with plenty of ruffles and a hat to match. Mr. Allen was wearing his black broadcloth suit with black riding boots and a black fedora hat.

They walked toward the church entrance. They saw several other families that had just parked their rigs doing the same. When they walked in the door and Mr. Allen removed his hat, the preacher was there greeting everyone. "Hello, Mr. Allen," he said as he shook his hand. "Good to see you could make it this morning."

"Hello, Parson Simmons," Mr. Allen returned. Parson Simmons greeted Louise and Vickie and shook hands with them too.

It was a bright, sunshiny day. The Allen family walked in and found a seat. They found a seat halfway down the aisle. They saw Jill and little Jacob when they sat down. They had to scoot down a little to make room for the Allen family.

"Hello, Jill," Vickie greeted as soon as she saw her. "And hi, Jacob," she said with a smile on her face. Jacob was such a cute little fella and was all dressed in a suit and tie. Jill was wearing her Sunday best also, which was always the same dress. But it was a dress with no patches in it. It was light pink and had been pressed to look really nice. She also had a hat the same shade as her dress. Everybody really dressed up when they came to church.

When it was time for the service to start, Parson Simmons walked down the aisle and stepped up to the pulpit. He started the service with a prayer as usual. Then the song leader got up and announced the page number of the hymn they would sing. There were songbooks on the back of each bench, so the Allen family pulled out a hymnbook as did Jill. Vickie had a high soprano voice, and so did Louise. But they found out that Jill sang a beautiful alto. And Mr. Allen had a deep bass voice. Little Jacob couldn't read yet and didn't know the words to any of the songs, but he knew the tune of each one. So he hummed the tune of each song. Everyone thought it was cute how Jacob was trying to sing.

After several songs, it was time for the sermon. And Parson Simmons was known for his long sermons. It took him an hour or so to get warmed up. Then it was about another hour before anyone had to stifle yawns, it seemed. But they endured it. The sermon lasted about three hours. Then everyone had to suppress the sigh of relief they felt when it was finally over.

They then sang the invitational hymn and had their closing prayer. Then everyone walked outside to start visiting with their fellow Christians.

"How are you?" Vickie asked when she finally got a chance to talk to Jill.

"Why, I'm fine," she said. "I haven't seen you here at church in several weeks."

"Yes, we don't come to church when we have trail driving crews going by. We have to keep the store open so they can replenish their supplies while on their way north."

"I can understand that," Jill said.

Vickie didn't really know Jill all that well, but she enjoyed talking to her. The members of the congregation apparently enjoyed the after-church fellowship maybe more than the church service itself, but no one let on.

When it came time for the crowd to break up and go back to their carriages, Vickie asked Louise, "Can I invite Jill and Jacob to have dinner with us?"

"Why, sure," Louise told her.

"Would you and Jacob like to have Sunday dinner with us?" she asked after she walked back over to where Jill and Jacob were standing.

"Why, I guess that would be okay." She asked Jacob, "Would you like to have Sunday dinner with the Allen family?"

"Yes!" he said. He knew they wouldn't have any kids his age to play with, but he liked the idea of a change. Just to get to visit someone would be a treat for him.

So Jill untied her rig and steered her horse behind the Allen carriage. When they reached the Allen place, Mr. Allen unhitched Jill's horse first and led him into the stall. Then he unharnessed his own rig. He pumped some water into the water trough and then put out some grain for the horses to eat. He didn't want to climb up in the barn loft to fork them down hay in his Sunday clothes, but he figured they needed mainly grain anyway.

When they walked into the yard, Jacob saw Scamp, who was jumping around, greeting everyone. "You have a dog!" he exclaimed.

"Yes, his name is Scamp," Vickie told him.

Jacob squatted down to pet him, and Scamp went wild. He wasn't accustomed to this much attention from this many people. When they went into the house, Jacob found out Scamp had to stay outside. "Why can't he come in the house, too?" he asked.

"Dogs aren't allowed in the house," Louise explained. She figured she had enough problems without having to deal with a dog trying to steal food from the table, and this way, they didn't have to house-train him.

Jacob finally accepted it and came on into the house with everyone else, leaving Scamp in the backyard. Louise and Vickie started cooking dinner, and Jill, of course, volunteered to help. So while the women were frying chicken and making mashed potatoes, Abe and little Jacob sat in the living room. At first, Jacob appeared sort of shy, being around strangers.

"Ever been fishing?" Mr. Allen asked him.

"No. There's no one to take me," he answered in a rather dejected manner.

"Well, now, the next time we go, you can go with us," Mr. Allen assured him.

"Really?" He had the boy's interest.

"Sure." Then Mr. Allen started talking to him about a fishing trip he had gone on in times past. He elaborated on one particular fish he had caught.

"It was this long," he said, holding his hands about two feet apart. Abe Allen hadn't been fishing in years. But had always enjoyed fishing in his youth.

"Do you think I could catch a fish like that?" Jacob asked him with an amazed look on his little face.

"I'm sure you could." Mr. Allen was already kind of regretting his offer because he normally never had time to fish these days. But he might fit in a trip to one of the creeks just so Jacob would get a chance to fish. He liked to take Louise and Vickie on picnics occasionally, and they could have a picnic near a creek.

When dinner was ready, Vickie walked into the living room to notify Mr. Allen and Jacob. So they got up and walked into the kitchen.

Mr. Allen said the blessing, and then they started eating. "Oh, boy!" exclaimed Jacob. "Fried chicken!"

"Now, mind your manners," cautioned Jill.

Everyone was hungry, so they started eating.

"So what do you do these days?" asked Vickie.

"I have a goat farm."

"What?" Her answer caught Vickie completely by surprise.

"Yes, my husband was killed in the war, but he left me this farm. We kept a few dairy goats because I liked goat's milk and goat butter. But I always kept all the nanny goats that were born and let them grow up and made milk goats out of them. I sold all the billy goats as soon as I could find someone to buy them. But by keeping all the nanny goats, the size of the herd built up, and I didn't want to have to milk that many goats. When trail drives pass through, if the cows have any calves, the cowboys always shoot the calves since they can't keep up with their mothers on the drive."

"They do?" Vickie was horrified.

"Yes, so I take my wagon and go up to the herd and see if they'll let me have the baby calves. They always give them to me. So I take them to my farm and let the nanny goats adopt a calf each. Then I don't have to milk them, but when the calf grows up, it's worth some money. Goats aren't worth anything when they grow up."

"That is amazing!" Vickie said.

"Did you ever go up to the Bennett herd?" Vickie then was very curious.

"I did go get some baby calves from a herd. When I asked the cook, he said he'd have to find out from the boss if I could have the calves. The boss's name was Jim."

"Was Jim killing baby calves?" she then asked, still shocked at the idea.

"No. The other cowboys were the ones shooting the calves. Jim was the one that told the other cowboys to stop killing them. He told them to just reach down and pull the calf up and lay it over his saddle and bring it to the chuck wagon. They tied the feet of the calves and put them in my wagon. So I have a pasture full of nanny goats with adopted baby calves now. I baked five apple pies for them and traded them for the calves."

Vickie had never heard of such, and it was all very interesting to her.

After they finished their visit, Mr. Allen went out and harnessed up her wagon; and she and little Jacob headed back to their farm. "I have to make sure the goats and calves have feed and water," she said.

CHAPTER 29

Running Mustangs Again

They started seeing herds of wild mustangs. They'd stampede as soon as they saw the mounted men. They were approaching the place where they had built a trap the previous winter. They found their old camp and settled down for the night.

The following morning, they were up at dawn having breakfast. After breakfast, Mark went out to take charge of the horse herd so the night guard could come in and eat. Then after breakfast, Jim and eight cowboys saddled up and rode down to inspect the trap. He Who Flies rode with them, but he didn't use a saddle, just a saddle blanket. They had placed the chuck wagon and set up camp several miles from the trap. Jim didn't want any human smell near the trap because you couldn't be sure which direction the wind would come from when they started running mustangs. But Jim wanted to see if it needed any repair work done. He hadn't seen it since the previous winter.

The trap was in good shape. Apparently, nothing had been there since it was last used. So Jim decided they would go seeking wild horses the following the morning. He wanted to let the horses rest at least a day first.

Jim was able to benefit from his experience the previous winter because he knew where to ride to avoid the mustangs until they were in position for a good run. He didn't want the mustangs to know they were even there until they could stampede them toward their trap.

Before leaving the chuck wagon that morning, Ben had told Jim he thought he should go and get some camp meat. Jim agreed, so Ben rode back to the east, where they had seen a herd of buffalo on their ride in. He took a couple of the cowboys with him to help him with the skinning and butchering. By the middle of the afternoon, they came back with a fat buffalo calf. It had been quartered and the meat divided up and tied behind their saddles.

Jim briefed the men on the coming mustang run that night. He would leave Mark to hold their horse herd, and of course, Charlie would be left behind to have them a meal ready when they got back. The next morning, when it was still dark, he led his crew into position, which required about a twenty-mile ride. He Who Flies was in the crew. Jim was careful to keep his men downwind from where the mustangs were known to be, and they held their horses to an easy canter so they wouldn't use them up before they started the run.

Jim had the men spread out with about fifty yards or so between each rider, and they started out in an easy lope. As soon as they topped a rise, they saw a herd of mustangs. The stallion of the herd snorted and rounded up his mares and got them to running to the east— wrong direction. They just let them go. They knew they'd never turn them. They kept on riding southward toward the trap.

They flushed another herd on the next rise they topped, and this time, they stampeded to the west. No big deal; Jim had been through all of this before. Seemed like it was just chance that initially got them going the direction they wanted them to go. It was on the fifth bunch that they got them to going south. They were over to the east of the line of cowboys. Jim spurred his horse into a gallop and, with arm signals, encouraged the cowboys to his left to do the same and had the men swing to the left like the spoke of a large wagon wheel. It looked like they were trying to get the mustangs to move east. But Jim's ruse didn't work. The mustang herd turned north instead of south.

Jim waved at the men to head back south instead of north. He knew they'd never catch them. It was nearly noon by then, so Jim decided to go to the chuck wagon and have dinner. It was time to change to fresh mounts anyway.

After they had dinner and each cowboy had roped a fresh horse, they started out again—this time, toward the east. Jim thought they might have better luck if they didn't work the same area each time. After going several miles, he found out they were actually angling toward the northeast due to the lay of the land, but that was okay. They wanted to make a circle anyway.

They rode up over a rise and flushed a herd of antelope. That didn't surprise Jim. He knew there were lots of antelope out here. They always herded together separate from the mustangs.

Then, after riding probably another hour, when they rode over a rise, they did flush a herd of mustangs. They ran to the northwest this time. So Jim and his crew just turned and followed them as if they wanted to drive them to the northwest. They held back and gave them plenty of room, but over each rise, they stampeded again. After five miles or so, the mustang herd took a turn to the south. Jim thought they might do that if the horse critters got the idea that that wasn't the direction they wanted them to go. Within a few minutes, they had fanned out, following the mustangs right toward the trap! Jim got a glimpse of the stallion in a herd—a buckskin. And he was beautifully built! Oh! But he hoped he could catch this stallion and keep him!

They kept riding, and the mustangs kept up their run to the south. At one point, Jim thought they might shift as the stallion tossed his head up and sniffed the air. But the men that were now near him waved their hats, and he kept running. So the mustang stallion just nipped a couple of mares on the rump to get them to go faster and started pulling away from the cowboys.

Just before they ran into the trap, the buckskin turned and headed straight for Jim, his jaws open, pure hatred in his eyes. Jim had already pulled the thong off his six-shooter as they approached the trap to be ready. He had his gun out ready to shoot the stallion to save himself and his horse when he saw a rawhide rope settle around the stallion's neck. And He Who Flies left his mount and ran along-side the stallion, pulling in the rope until he succeeded in choking him down, and then threw him. He had his front feet hobbled before he could get up. He had no saddle horn to fasten the rope to, so he had to just handle the rope by hand.

All the mares were in the trap by then, so Jim spurred his horse to get even more speed out of him; and he dismounted at the gate and put the two rails up and draped the blanket over them.

But Jim was astounded at the actions of the Comanche. After he had hobbled the stallion's front feet, he allowed him to get up. Then the stallion immediately charged him again. But the hobbles held his front feet, and he tumbled to the ground again. He let him up and just repeated this process over and over until the stallion was exhausted. Then he pulled on the rope, stretching his neck tight so he couldn't reach him with those powerful jaws, put one hand over his eyes, and breathed into his nostrils. The stallion seemed to relax almost instantly. Then, keeping his eyes covered, he breathed into his nostrils again. He took the rope from around his neck and fastened it around his lower jaw.

He then removed the stallion's hobbles, allowed him to get up and led him around several minutes. The stallion was completely subdued. He mounted the stallion and rode him up to Jim and said, "Good horse." Jim was still awestruck at seeing what seemed to him impossible! He thought for sure he'd have to kill the stallion to save himself and his horse. If he had ever seen killer instinct in an animal's eyes, he had seen it in the stallion when he charged him.

They rode up to the trap to see if they could get a count of the mares they had gathered. The mares were still milling around but were tired enough that they had slowed down. Jim managed to get a count of his catch. There were thirty-three mares and twenty-seven colts—not bad at all.

He Who Flies then offered to sell the stallion to Jim. Since he had caught and tamed it, he considered the stallion to be his own property. Jim asked him how much. "Ten dollars," He Who Flies answered.

Jim immediately reached back into his saddlebags for his money bag and counted out ten silver dollars and handed them to He Who Flies. He wanted the buckskin for stud purposes.

He Who Flies was still astride the buckskin stallion. "You need to breathe into his nostrils too so he'll know you are also his master," he said. He Who Flies dismounted and put his hands over the stallion's eyes. So Jim breathed into his nostrils twice. The buckskin snorted the first time. Then he calmed down.

Jim took the two bars down from the gate, and He Who Flies led the stallion into the trap. He then took the rope from his lower lip and allowed him to herd with the mares. He was a tame horse now. Jim put the two bars back up and draped the blanket over them again.

It was time for dinner, so the men rode the several miles to the chuck wagon. Charlie had chuck ready. After they ate, each puncher roped and saddled a fresh horse then rode back to the trap.

That afternoon, they roped each mare and colt, threw them, tied their tail to one of the front feet, and then let them up. After they finished hobbling all of them, they opened the gate and ran them into the herd of tame horses. Jim had the herd of mares he wanted and to have such an excellent stud to go with them was an invaluable bonus!

The mustangs were thirsty, so they went to the creek for a drink, first of all. Then they settled down to grazing with the tame horses. They fought their hobbles at first but were hungry, so they didn't fight them long.

Jim still wanted some saddle horses. So the following morning, they rode out again, seeking a bachelor herd. They found several herds that spooked and ran different directions before they finally found one with stallions only. But they didn't run toward the trap. Jim had figured out that this job required mountains of patience.

They rode the rest of that day and stampeded lots of mustangs and a couple of herds of antelope. At the end of the day, they headed back to the chuck wagon.

It was two days later when they flushed a herd of bachelor mustangs. It was about midmorning, and they managed to get them headed toward the trap. Jim noticed a lot of strawberry roans in the bunch. That was okay. He knew they would make good saddle horses.

They ran into the trap, and Jim got the panels on the gate up and the blanket draped across it. So they had their herd of bachelor broncs now too! They made a count of the herd and found out they had forty-seven horses in this bunch.

The next day, they decided that five of the bachelor broncs were scrubs and turned them loose. Then they built a fire and got the branding irons started on heating. They stepped through the panels of the fence and started branding the new horses. Jim just branded them with the Slant JB brand this time. They roped and threw each one and one of the cowpunchers brought them a branding iron and Jim changed each one to a gelding. Then Ben tied a rope to each bronc's front foot and the other end to a back foot. Then they let him up and roped another. After two days, they were done with the branding, and the horses were ready to be turned out. They went to the creek to get water first; then they joined the horse herd.

It was three days later that they broke camp and got their horse herd started to the east, toward civilization and out of Indian country.

CHAPTER 30

Horse Thieves

They headed out at first light eastward toward the place Jim had picked out to start his ranch. Jim had provided He Who Flies with a mount except He Who Flies still refused to use a saddle. He just tied a rope to his lower lip, put a blanket on his back, and mounted up.

"Guide horse with knees," he explained.

"Do you want a bridle or hackamore? I have more of them in the chuck wagon," Jim said.

"No," He Who Flies answered. He said he could use the rope on the horse's lower lip to halt it with.

Jim knew they were in luck from the fact that they hadn't seen any Indians so far on this trip—other than He Who Flies of course. And he knew they couldn't count on being so lucky. So he decided to double the guard on the horses each night. That meant the men wouldn't get as much sleep, but he thought it was better to get less sleep than to be dead.

After three days' travel, Jim got the idea that maybe the Indians weren't going to bother them after all. They camped that night, and all was quiet. He considered the idea of going back to just two-night herders for the horses.

When they camped that night, it was an especially dark night. There was no moon, and a solid overcast obscured the stars. And there was no wind. All was quiet except for the occasional hooting of an owl in the distance, and sometimes, they'd hear a coyote howl. But they were normal sounds.

It wasn't until after midnight that Jim woke up. At first, he couldn't figure out what woke him up. Then he figured it out. All was quiet—no night sounds. He immediately got up and stamped on his boots and buckled on his gun belt. He went to his night horse and mounted up. He saw He Who Flies was already astride his horse on the edge of camp.

"It isn't Indians," He Who Flies said quietly.

Jim looked at him—looked at his voice. It was too dark to see his face. "But there's someone out there," Jim muttered. It was more of a question than a statement.

"Yes. White men."

Then all hell broke loose. The attackers came from the west with guns blazing. They could see the gun flashes as the horse thieves approached. They rode by and shot up the camp. In the darkness, it was pure chance if they hit anything, but Jim pulled out his rifle and started firing at the gun flashes. He Who Flies had taken his bow from his back and was shooting arrows at them. The attackers fired at the chuck wagon and at the sleeping forms, but the men came out of their blankets very quickly and rushed to their night horses.

Of course, the horse herd stampeded almost immediately with the noise. The men had to mount up without their boots but had to take time to buckle on their gun belts and tighten the cinches of their saddles before they raced after the sound of the stampeding horses. Each cowboy had to give his horse his head because a horse can see in the dark better than a man. It was the only way to avoid running into a tree or off into a gully or such.

But they lost the horse herd. Since they couldn't see them, they couldn't follow them. Jim finally called a halt. He told the men they'd find them in the morning. So they rode back to camp and returned to their blankets. Jim checked to see if anyone had been hit by the random gunfire during the attack. One cowboy had a graze on his shoulder; and another one had been hit in the leg, but it was only a flesh wound. Jim put bandages on the wounded men before they turned in to get some sleep.

They were up at sunup, following the tracks of the stolen herd. Jim had stuffed a small sack of flour and some buffalo beef into a flour sack and put it in his saddlebags before they left. The practice of keeping their night horses tied and mounting them to ride after the stampeding herd was all that kept them from being left completely afoot.

They followed the tracks of the stolen horse herd all day. Jim could tell they were gaining on them because the tracks started looking fresher. They held their horses back to a steady trot to save them since they had no replacement mounts. They hobbled their horses so they could graze that night and restore some of their energy. They camped near a creek so they would have water.

Since their horses did get some rest during the night, they decided they could push on the next morning. Jim knew that the stolen herd would be exhausted after their initial run and would have to have more rest than their own mounts since they hadn't pushed them.

The next morning, after a quick breakfast of buffalo meat and biscuits, they put out the fire, saddled up, and resumed their pursuit of the stolen horses. Before they had left the camp the previous morning, Jim had told the cook, "You'll have to camp here until we recover the horses. We'll bring back the work horses as soon as we reclaim them so you can move the chuck wagon." So the cook and the cook's flunky remained in camp.

Jim noticed the tracks were getting fresher. So they were able to make time on the stolen horse herd.

They finally overtook the horse herd shortly after noon. They were gathered in a bunch, and the horses were exhausted. Jim knew that the best time to attack was immediately before the horse thieves even knew they had been caught up with.

Jim sent four men out to take out the horse guards. Then Jim, Ben, and the rest of the Slant JB crew rode into camp with their guns blazing. Three horse thieves fell to the fire of their guns. Two of them got away. But Jim got a glimpse of the face of one of the thieves. It was Jeb, one of the men he had fired when he refused to eat at the same fire as He Who Flies!

So it was Jeb and Gene who stole the herd! They had apparently recruited some horse thieves to help them. Jim spurred his horse in the direction of the two fleeing riders. He didn't intend to let any of them get away.

The horse herd had stampeded again, but this time, toward the west. So they were heading back toward their own camp. Ben was riding at his elbow. They pulled their horses to a walk to save them and just followed the tracks of the horse thieves. They were determined to get them. All the cowboys had followed them.

They stopped at noon to cook a meal and rest their horses. After they had dinner, Jim told Mark and three of the cowboys to go find the horse herd, gather them up, and just let them graze but to rope the two workhorses, put halters on them, and lead them back to the chuck wagon. The chuck wagon should catch up to them in a day or so. The remaining five cowboys would continue to look for the horse thieves.

They kept following the tracks of the retreating thieves. They couldn't keep up this pace forever. They'd kill their horses if they did. But they followed at an easy lope. They reached a rocky area and slowed their horses to a walk. The trail led down to a creek. The horse tracks led down into the creek but didn't come out on the other side. Jim had used that trick before. They'd have to follow the banks of the creek probably for miles both ways to find out where they came out.

"I can take half the men and check the creek banks to the north, and you can take the other half and check them to the south," Ben suggested.

Jim knew it could take days before they picked up their trail again. And he didn't want to spend the time on it. "We'll ride on back to the horse thieves' camp and bury the dead," Jim decided.

When they got back to the horse thieves' campfire, there were four dead men lying on the ground. They had no shovels to dig graves with. They were at the chuck wagon. But they took the time to search them. One of them had a Colt that fired metal cartridges. Jim decided to keep it. He put his cap-and-ball revolver in his saddlebags for use as another spare gun. He had two cap-and-ball revolvers. One he had already been keeping in his saddlebags for a spare and the other one he carried in a holster at his belt. But the Colt he took off the dead body of the horse thief fired .44 cartridges as did his rifle. He Who Flies picked up one of the rifles of the rustlers off the ground. Jim nodded to him it was okay for him to keep it. Then Jim and his crew retrieved all the ammunition from the dead bodies that they found, and then they covered each one's face with a saddle blanket. They'd bury them when the chuck wagon caught up with them.

CHAPTER 31

Jim Homesteads 2,048 Acres

After the chuck wagon caught up with them, Jim and the Slant JB crew headed the horse herd to the place that Jim had chosen to make his homestead. It was about twenty miles or so to the west of the place where Jack's ranch was located. It was a place that was about one mile wide (east and west) and three miles long (north and south). It had a creek running across it on a diagonal, going from the northeast to the southwest. So it had plenty of water, and there was good grass on both sides of the creek.

Jim had stopped at the courthouse and read up on the homestead law on one of his trips to Waco the previous spring. He had learned that you can homestead 160 acres if you intend to farm it, but you can homestead 2,048 acres if you intend it for grazing only.

When they reached the spot Jim had picked out to homestead, they halted the horse herd, and Jim explained his intentions to the men.

"We're going to build a corral first. We need to saddle break the geldings we have caught. Then I intend to build a barn, a cabin, and a rail fence around the entire 2,048 acres." The plantations in the South where Jim grew up all had rail fences around their boundary, so this seemed the natural thing to do.

Jim knew that cowboys didn't like to work off the back of a horse. So he explained to them that they could start rounding up cattle, and they could brand any calves they saw running with a mother that had a Slant JB brand. The boys that had joined the outfit as greenies were mostly farm boys who had prior experience building things like barns, cabins, and pens. They were willing to work with their hands.

So Jim separated out the men according to their skills, and he would have liked to have some more men. But he figured he could make do with the crew he had for now until he got a chance to go to the nearest town.

"Ben, will you take over as foreman? Your pay will increase to forty-five dollars a month."

"Sure," Ben said.

"Okay, then take the chuck wagon and cook with you and start a roundup. Brand any mavericks you find and turn them loose."

When Ben and the cowboys left, Jim took the greenies and got started felling trees to make logs—first to use for building a corral, then a barn. The cabin would be next after that.

Jim decided he'd better make the trip to town right away to file on his homestead. And he would see if he could hire some more hands while he was there. Besides, they needed supplies. They were starting to run low on grub.

Jim put a couple of pack saddles on two of the horses and saddled up the dapple gray to ride. He was turning out to be a pretty good horse. He started his ride to the town of Killeen, which he knew to be the county seat. It was about a twenty-mile ride.

When he arrived in town, he went to the county courthouse first and filed his claim. He found out he had to have some way to measure distance and then to place an oak post in each corner of his property. But he could file it based on the landmarks. A major bend in the creek as shown on the county clerk's map identified his northern boundary. The four corners of his place could be measured from there.

Jim rode over to the saloon to see if there was anyone wanting work. He didn't see anyone but a couple of professional gamblers. So he rode over to the general store and bought the supplies he needed. He asked the storekeeper if there was anyone around looking for work.

The storekeeper did know of a family in which the father had been killed by a horse falling on him. He had two teenage boys that would probably be willing to work for a few months.

So when Ben rode back to his new ranch, he had several weeks' worth of supplies, a certificate of homestead for his place, and two new hands that had experience building log cabins. The oldest boy said he and his brother had helped their father build the log cabin they were living in.

When they arrived at the homestead, Jim put the two new boys to work building a bunkhouse. Then they'd need a cookshack, then a barn, and after that, a cabin. The corral was nearly finished. Jim loaded some chuck onto a packhorse and saddled his buckskin gelding and went out to find the chuck wagon crew. He knew they were low on flour and out of bacon. So he wanted to bring them some grub. He also wanted to just check on them too.

It took a day of searching to find the chuck wagon. He saw a plume of smoke late in the evening and rode up to find their campfire going and the cook cooking supper. He unloaded the supplies, which included two sides of bacon, a sack of beans, a sack of flour, and a sack of spuds. He also brought coffee and a couple of cartons of Bull Durham tobacco.

When everyone was seated around the campfire but the night guard, he said, "I filed a claim, so the ranch is now legally mine. The corral is now finished, and a barn is being built. I want two men to work as full-time bronc busters. Anyone interested?"

Immediately, four men raised their hands. "I only need two," Jim said. "Ted and Will have been with me the longest. They'll be our new bronc busters."

Jim unrolled his bedroll and slept on the ground near the other men that night. The next morning, Jim found out they had eggs for breakfast. Where did they get the eggs?

"Where did the eggs come from?" Jim asked the cook.

"A girl came riding up in a buckboard with a bucket of eggs to sell," he answered.

"Which direction did she come from?" was Jim's next question.

"From the north."

Every man had half a dozen fried eggs with their biscuits and bacon—a real treat! When Jim, Ted, and Will saddled up to leave, Jim decided he'd find out where the girl came from. Instead of going south to the ranch, they headed north.

After about a two-hour ride, they saw a plume of smoke rising above some trees along the creek bank. They rode on into the trees and found a cabin, barn, and corral. Then they saw a cornfield with a man, three boys, and two girls out hoeing. It had a rail fence around it.

The three men rode up to the fence and halted. The man saw them and walked over. "Howdy," he said.

"Well, howdy," Jim replied.

"Gotta hoe the corn. Keep the weeds out of it," he said.

"Yeah," Jim said. "Looks like I'm going to be your neighbor. I'm starting a ranch about fifteen miles or so south of here."

"Why, glad to meet you. My name's Ollie. These are my kids."

"I'm Jim, and these two are Ted and Will." He pointed at the two men on either side of him.

"If you need any eggs or cured pork, Ma's at the house."

"Well, now we appreciate the eggs you brought over last night. It's good to have eggs at the chuck wagon. And at the cook house at ranch headquarters too."

"We raise chickens and have a hen house full of laying hens. Figured eggs would sell good around here."

"They certainly do."

"We need to be going. Got work to do, but it was good to meet you," Jim said in parting. Then he and the two cowboys rode off.

When they arrived at the ranch and rode to the corral, Jim said, "We're going to break the horses the Indian way. He Who Flies will show you how."

They had seen the miracle the Indian had performed on the killer stallion. Neither of them had any argument.

They had forty-two mustangs that needed to be saddle broke. He walked up to He Who Flies. "Will you show these two men how to saddle break a horse the Indian way?"

"Yes" was all He Who Flies said.

When Jim was a boy in South Carolina, they gently broke their horses. They lived on a plantation and raised mostly cotton, but they wanted horses for jumping and fox hunting. They broke them without ever allowing them to buck a single time, but it took about six months to break a horse that way. He really was glad he had learned of a way to saddle break a bronc in such a short period of time.

With Ted and Will sitting on the corral fence watching, He Who Flies roped one of the roan geldings with his rawhide lariat. He roped his front legs so when the gelding charged him, he sidestepped and threw him. He let him up but had left the rope on his front legs. The gelding charged him again. He sidestepped and pulled hard on the rope and threw him again. He got up and charged him again. He threw him each time he charged him. He kept working him till he was tired enough that before letting him up, he could pull the rope tight, put his hands over his eyes, and breath into his nostrils. He breathed into his nostrils several times before he let him up again. When the gelding got to his feet again, he no longer seemed eager to fight. So He Who Flies fastened a piece of piggin' string to his lower lip, removed the rope from his legs, and just led him around. Occasionally, he would stop and stroke his neck and back. The gelding seemed gentle but still a little skittish. After a couple of hours, He Who Flies was astride the roan and riding him around the corral. Will and Ted were both flabbergasted. But each of them roped a bronc and imitated He Who Flies's actions.

So instead of taking a month to rough break a herd of horses, they had the entire cavvy of forty-two mustangs saddle broke and gentled down inside a week. Then Jim also thought about how he should get all the mustangs that had just been saddle broke shod. He had helped Jack shoe mustangs, but he had no blacksmith shop; so he had the horse breakers take the freshly broke mustangs to the closest town—four at a time—to get them shoes. They needed to be ridden daily anyway. Two of the mustangs they'd ride, and each cowboy could lead another one. Then they'd change saddles before heading back so the other two horses could get some more time under the saddle. If He Who Flies went along, they would get six horses shod instead of four. And they could make two trips a day; so after about a week and a half, all the new broncs had shoes.

When the barn was finished, he assigned the two men that had built it to helping the two newly hired boys with the bunkhouse and cookshack. When they were finished, he got them started on the rail fence that was to go around the boundary of his property. He rode out to check on the branding crew again. Ben explained to him that they were finding a lot of Bar OB and Slant BB cattle among his own. There were a few of Jack's Rolling JW cattle too. Jim just cautioned him to not brand any calf that wasn't weaned unless it was nursing a Slant JB cow. Ben asked him about maverick cattle, and Jim said to go ahead and brand them if he was sure they were weaned.

After the rail fence around the property was completed, Jim had Mark run the mares and the buckskin stallion into the pasture. He explained that the fenced area would be their horse pasture. They'd still let the cattle run on the open range.

After the branding crew had branded all the Slant JB calves and any mavericks a year old and up within about a ten-mile radius of the JB Ranch, Jim decided it was time to go hunt wild cattle again. It was August by then, and he figured he had time to make one more drive to Kansas.

Jim left three men to hold the ranch and watch the herd of mares. He loaded up the chuck wagon and took his cavvy of riding horses and headed back to West Texas to make another gather of wild cattle.

CHAPTER 32

Another Wild Cow Hunt

After three days' travel, they started seeing a few wild cattle in the distance. But Jim decided to keep going a day or two longer to see if they could find some bigger herds. When Jim started seeing herds of cattle big enough in size to be worthwhile, they stopped and made camp.

At the campfire that night, Jim explained to the crew, "When we first see wild cattle, they will stampede as soon as they see us. That's okay. We'll just follow them and let them run. Have a canteen on your saddle and some cold biscuits in your pocket. We'll have to run all day and all night without stopping. Mark will keep the horses up close enough that you can stop and rope a fresh horse every three hours or so. You'll kill your horse if you don't.

"We'll have to run them one day and a night and all the next day at least, maybe longer before we can settle them down enough to start herd breaking them. We have to wait until they're tired enough. But don't let them bed down during the day. We want to get them good and tired so we can herd break them.

"And take the thong off your six-shooter as soon as you start the run. If a wild critter charges your horse with those long horns, you may have to shoot him to save your horse. If you can get a crazy longhorn in between two cowpunchers and both of you rope him, you have a chance of saving the cow critter without danger of getting yourself or your horse killed. If the cows with small calves want to fall behind with their calves, let them. We mainly want bulls. We'll make steers out of them and drive them to Kansas. We ride out at daybreak."

The following morning, they started out. They saw several bunches right off, and of course, the wild cattle spooked and ran off. They followed them as they started their run.

The punchers gave the herd plenty of distance per Jim's instructions to minimize the chances of having a herd quitter go after their horses. But one bull quit the herd anyway and headed toward Jim's horse. Jim had his loop out but had to maneuver his horse to avoid getting gored. The bull followed him and would have stuck one of those long horns in his horse's side if Ben's loop hadn't settled on the bull's horns just in time. The bull hit the end of the rope and turned a half somersault.

He bawled loudly and angrily and got up to charge Ben's horse. Jim got his loop on his horns just in time and turned his horse so his back was to the bull. The bull turned another half somersault. When he got up, they both held their ropes tight so he couldn't charge either horse, but he kept on fighting. They didn't try to shake the loop loose from his horns.

Waylon saw what was going on and rode up from behind the bull and roped his front feet. Jim and Ben then slacked their ropes enough so that he could charge them again. This time, when the bull turned a half somersault, he couldn't get up because Waylon's horse was holding the rope tight. Waylon hopped off his horse and ran around to the bull's back. He took his piggin' string, leaned over, and tied the bull's feet.

Jim and Ben then left their loops slack so the bull could breathe. They didn't want a dead bull. Waylon got out his knife and changed him to a steer.

After that, when Waylon mounted his horse with one end of the piggin' string in his hand so he could yank on it and free the steer's feet, he let him up. He seemed somewhat subdued. So Jim and Ben both slacked their ropes and Ben yanked his rope free from the steer's horns and then Jim did so too. The steer ambled on back toward the herd. It took a lot to take the fight out a mean longhorn.

They kept the rest of the cattle running all day. When Jim got thirsty, he took a drink from his canteen. And he was grateful for the biscuits in his pocket. He could eat a biscuit occasionally and stave off the pangs of hunger a little while longer.

When night fell, the cattle kept on running. Jim's legs felt like rubber. When it finally got to be daylight, Jim was really weary. In fact, he was exhausted. But they kept the herd running. If they got them tired enough, herd breaking would be possible.

The greenies found out what it was like to have to ride for two days and one night straight with no sleep and no rest. They still changed horses every three hours so they wouldn't kill them.

It was late in the evening when the cattle finally stopped. When the cowboys let them start milling, Jim noticed that they didn't have as big a gather as he expected. When the chuck wagon caught up and got a pot of coffee brewing, each man came to the fire for coffee and a plate of grub. The coffee was ready first, of course, but the beef, beans, and biscuits soon followed.

The cattle were tired enough that they bedded down with no problem. Jim assigned four cowboys to night guard. The other cowboys went to bed and were very grateful to finally get some sleep. Night guard lasted two hours, then they rode in and woke up their relief. So each cowboy only got six hours of sleep. They were still tired when morning came.

After breakfast, Jim went out and made a count of the longhorns. Jim found out he only had 532 wild cattle. He decided to take the time right then to make steers out of the bulls.

Jim had two of the cowboys cut the bulls out of the herd one at a time and had another cowboy rope the bull's front feet. Then a third cowboy was on hand to jump out of his saddle and go tie the bull's feet. Then a fourth cowboy was there with his knife out to cut off the bull's testicles. Jim knew they would be easier to handle after they'd been cut.

After that, they finished herd breaking them. Jim left four men to guard the cattle while they went looking for some more. They did find several bunches of cattle, but they also saw some branded stock among them—quite a few branded with the Bar BB brand, but there were other brands too. So Jim finally figured out that the frontier had been pushed farther west faster than he had expected. He decided to wind up the wild cow hunt. He still had money in the bank at Waco. He could buy enough steers to make a big enough herd for another drive.

But they did haze all the mavericks that they found into their herd. They took their small herd, about 750 head by this time, and headed them eastward to Jim's new ranch. Jim rode to the county seat again. It had a bank. He wrote a draft on his Waco account and got the money he needed to buy cattle with. Then Jim took four men and stopped at farms and any ranch he came to along the way to see if they had any steers they wanted to sell. He decided he would have to range farther south to find enough cattle to make a herd. He wanted only steers. Grown cattle were selling for three dollars a head that summer.

The next morning, a buckboard pulled up to the cookshack and stopped. A girl fastened the brake and then got down. She got two buckets out of the back and walked in. She asked the cook, "Would you like to buy some eggs?" She showed him the two buckets.

"Why, yes," Cookie said. "Where did you get them?"

"From our hens. We have a whole pen full of chickens. I'm Becky from the Harper farm."

"Why, glad to meet you," Cookie replied and took the eggs. He got out a sack from his grub box and paid her.

Then Becky went out to her rig and climbed in. She undid the hand brake and drove off.

Putting a Herd Together

Before looking for cattle to the south, Jim decided to go by Jack's ranch and pay him a visit. He might want to sell some steers by now. He left Ben in charge of the herd and took three men with him this time. He rode up to Jack's ranch and hailed the cookshack. He figured the cook would at least be there and know where Jack would be.

The cook came to the door and looked out. He recognized Jim. "Why, light down and come in for some coffee," the cook called out. The four men dismounted and tied their horses to the hitch rail. They walked into the cookshack and accepted a cup of coffee. They'd been riding most of the morning.

"And where might Jack be?" Jim asked after taking a sip of his coffee.

"Out branding cattle," answered the cook. "They've been branding all summer."

"Can you tell me where to find their chuck wagon?" Jim then asked.

"Sure. It's over to the southwest by now probably. So you're needin' to talk to Jack?" The cook was curious.

"We're starting a drive north. I figured I'd see if he had any steers ready to sell."

"I'm sure he does," the cook then said.

So after having coffee, the men each rolled a smoke and then went out, remounted, and headed toward the southwest. After riding an hour or so, they saw dust above the horizon and rode toward it.

Sure enough, after another hour or so, they saw a herd of cattle in the distance. Jim looked up at the sun and decided it was about noon.

They rode up to the chuck wagon and hailed the cook. "Hello, the fire," Jim called out.

The cook looked up and said, "Hello. State your business."

"Want to talk to Jack," Jim said.

"He'll be riding in for dinner in just a little bit."

Jim and his men dismounted and tied their horses to two of the wagon wheels. They went to the fire and poured a cup of coffee each. They figured they might as well have coffee while they were waiting.

After a few minutes, men started riding in. They each put their horse in the rope corral and unsaddled him, then came to the fire to get chuck. When Jim saw Jack, he stood up and put out his hand.

"Why, hello, Jim. It's good to see you. Where have you been?"

"Out gathering wild stuff," Jim answered. "And it's good to see you."

Jack filled a cup with coffee and got a plate of food from the tailgate of the wagon. "Help yourself to some chuck," Jack said. Jim and his men did so. Then they sat down and started eating.

"I didn't get as good a gather as we did last year. So I'm out looking for steers to buy. Getting ready for another drive north," Jim explained. He knew Jack would be curious.

"The frontier has been pushed farther west now that the war's over. It'll be harder to find enough wild cattle to make a herd," Jack said.

"Yeah. Wondered if you had any steers you wanted to sell this year."

"Well, now we do have. We're still branding mavericks, but a lot of them are big enough to go to Kansas. I just decided to spend this summer branding so we can get it caught up. We have had problems with rustlers around here."

"I'll buy all you want to sell," Jim said.

"What we can start doing is just moving all the four-year-olds and older into a separate herd when we brand them. When you get ready to leave for Abilene, bring your cowboys over and add them to your herd."

"Okay. I'm going south to see if I can buy some more down there. On our way back, we'll stop by here and see how many you've got."

So after they'd finished eating, Jim and his men headed on south to look for more steers to buy. They got a bill of sale from each farmer and rancher they bought stock from. They managed to buy about one thousand and two hundred or so steers. Jim wanted only steers that were four years old or older. Then on the way back, he stopped by Jack's place and added another thousand head or so to the herd. He wrote him a check to pay him. Jack gave him a bill of sale. Jim found he only had about $1,000 or so left in the bank after he had finished buying cattle, but he figured that would be enough to get his herd to Abilene.

Jim finally managed to get together a herd of 2,945 steers. He decided that that would be enough to make a drive. In the herd were 382 cows, many of them with calves, and heifers that were still too young to calve. They allowed the cows with calves to lag behind and just had some of the cowboys stay behind to keep them bunched up, but some of them obviously caught up with them later. The calves running with their mothers were big enough this late in the summer that it was practical to keep them during the gather.

Then Jim had the men build a working chute in his corral so they could put his brand on his herd. They ran the cows and heifers through the chute first and branded them with the Slant JB before they started on the steers. They branded a slit across the existing brand on the ones they bought.

Some of the cowboys wanted to draw their wages and ramble. Jim paid them and went looking for drovers to replace them so he could get his new herd started north. He rode to any town he came to and stopped at each farmhouse to see if anyone wanted work.

He left three hands behind to stay at the bunkhouse and watch after his horse herd—Adam, Lee, and Alvin.

They separated out all the cows and calves this time. Jim wanted steers only. It was the latter part of August before he was ready to start his drive.

Vickie and Jill

Jill parked her rig in front of the Allen General store and walked in with little Jacob.

"I need some supplies," she told Vickie after they walked in.

"Well, it's good to see you! And we should have the supplies you need."

Jill showed her her shopping list. She wanted flour, cornmeal, beans, potatoes and a side of bacon. And she had brought in some eggs to sell. She had to go back out to her wagon and get another bucket full of them. While Vickie was helping gather up the things she needed, Mr. Allen came out of his office. He had heard them and recognized Jill's voice. He looked down at little Jacob and said, "We talked about going fishing, didn't we?"

"Yes!" he answered quickly. Mr. Allen had been thinking about how sad it was for the boy to not have a father to ever take him fishing.

"How would you like to come with our family on a picnic next Saturday?" he asked Jill.

"I'd like that a lot!" she said.

"We can have our picnic out near a creek, and Jacob can see if he can catch a fish or two."

"That would be wonderful!" exclaimed Jill.

Mr. Allen carried the flour, beans, and cornmeal out to the carriage. They were heavy. Then he gave her directions to the place where they'd have the picnic. It wasn't too far from her farm.

So the following Saturday, Abe Allen, Louise, and Vickie were unloading their carriage near a creek north of Waco. Vickie had left Scamp in the backyard when they left. She'd heard her father say he planned to show Jacob how to fish and thought he might be in the way. Abe got them a campfire going. Louise put on a pot of coffee to brew. She knew Abe would want coffee. While waiting for the coffee to brew, Abe took a hatchet from his carriage and chopped down a sapling. Then he got out his pocketknife and trimmed all the branches off it. It became obvious in a few minutes that he was making a fishing pole.

After the coffee was ready and Abe, Louise, and Vickie were sitting on a log near the fire sipping coffee, they heard a whip pop, and Jill drove up. Abe helped her down from the carriage and reached up to lift Jacob down. Then he unharnessed her mare and staked her out near his gelding.

Jill sat down at the fire to have a cup of coffee, and Abe showed Jacob the fishing pole he had made. "Okay!" he said. "Can I hold it?" So Abe let him hold the fishing pole. Then he got out some string to tie to the end of it and fastened a fishhook on the end of the string.

"We'll need some bait," Mr. Allen told him. "Can you catch us some grasshoppers?" Abe knew they'd find some grasshoppers if they went out looking for them. Abe managed to catch two grasshoppers, then Jacob caught one. He kept looking and caught three more. They put them in a bean can, and Abe put a lid over it fashioned out of rawhide.

So Abe gave Jacob his first fishing lesson while the women got dinner ready. He decided they needed something for a float, so he just took one of the chunks of wood he had left after making the fishing pole and tied it about two feet from the fishhook. Then he put a grasshopper on the hook and tossed it out into the creek and showed Jacob how to just watch the piece of wood. If it disappeared under the water, that meant he had a fish on the hook.

"I want to hold the pole!" said Jacob.

"You can hold the pole," Abe told him and handed it to him.

They hadn't had a bite yet when the women called them and told them dinner was ready. So Abe showed Jacob how to pull in the line and wrap it around the pole. He set it against a tree, and they went to the fire to eat. It was cold fried chicken this time with potato salad. Apparently, the only thing they intended the fire for was to make coffee.

"It sure is a beautiful day," Jill remarked as they started eating.

"It sure is," agreed Vickie.

"So you didn't catch a fish yet," Louise remarked.

"Not yet," responded Abe. He wasn't really very optimistic about catching any fish but he felt like he had to try. They'd try some more after dinner.

After the women cleaned up from dinner, they walked over to the creek. When Abe saw them coming, he got up and walked toward them. "Be real quiet," he cautioned them. "We don't want to spook the fish."

So the women ceased talking and walked up to see little Jacob holding the fishing pole watching the wooden float in the middle of the creek to see if it would disappear.

Then the float did disappear! "Pull it up," Abe said urgently to Jacob. Jacob did and saw a fish wiggling. Then the fish jumped loose and flopped back into the water.

"It got away," whined little Jacob.

"Yes, it did. When you get a bite, you have to lift it up and swing it over the bank quickly without letting your line go slack. If you aren't fast enough the fish does get away."

So Abe rebaited the hook so Jacob could toss it back into the water. It was probably ten or fifteen minutes before Jacob got another bite. Then Abe said, "Pull it up and swing it over the bank. Hurry."

Jacob did so this time and saw the wiggly, flapping fish on the grass. Abe immediately got the fish by the gills and removed the hook. He held the fish up so that Jacob could see it. Jacob was jumping up and down with excitement this time.

Abe went to the carriage and got out a one-gallon can and walked down to the creek and filled it with water. Then he popped in the fish. "This will keep it fresh until we get time to clean it," he explained. The fish was about five inches long.

He rebaited Jacob's hook and let him throw his line back into the creek. The women were entertained by Jacob's antics at first but then seemed to get bored and wandered off to look at the wildflowers, and they also wanted enough distance from the fishermen so they could talk. But Jill was especially happy that Jacob had someone to teach him to fish!

CHAPTER 35

Another Drive up the Trail

"We head the cattle north tomorrow," Jim told them at the campfire that night.

"I want to go home," said Willy. He was one of greenies they had hired. "I decided I like plowing better than riding. And we're near our farm."

"That's fine," Jim said. "You can draw your wages tomorrow morning before we head out. You can wait until we get near your place so you can ride a Slant JB horse to your home. We'll have a cowboy ride with you to bring back your horse." Jim knew his folks would be glad to see him, and he'd have money in his pocket now.

He Who Flies said, "I'll stay here. I can stay with the crew that watches the ranch. I can keep a watch over the horses."

"That is fine," Jack said. "Do you want the wages you've earned so far now?"

"I'd like to get paid in horses," He Who Flies answered.

So Jim agreed to pay him two horses for each month he had worked. That was twelve horses so far. He'd been with him about six months or so.

Several more of the cowboys drew their wages and quit. They were mostly greenies that decided they liked the life on the farm better than riding a horse all day. But a couple of them were experienced cowboys that just wanted to take their personal horses and ride to see new country. So Jim took what was left of the branding crew and the chuck wagon and started his herd of steers north. Ben Walker had proven himself a good foreman. Jim was glad that he decided to stay with the Slant JB and make the drive.

Jim intended to replace the men that quit, but he figured he could find more hands at Waco. He told the cook to let the store-keeper know they wanted more cowboys when he went in to replenish supplies.

As they neared Waco, Ben knew Jim would take time out to go visit Vickie again.

And Jim knew that Ben would want to pay a call on Jill as they drove the cattle by her place.

When Jim rode his gray up to the Allen store, he dismounted and tied his horse to the rail like normal. When he walked in, Vickie was waiting on a customer. Jim waited patiently until she had finished collecting the money for his purchases. Then she saw Jim. She ran around the counter as usual and tried to knock him down as usual. He swung her around as usual.

"Did you get a ranch started?" was the first question she asked.

"Yep," he said. He used a very casual tone of voice like as if a young man started a ranch every day.

"Did you find the horses you wanted?" was her next question, excitement in her voice.

He explained about the herd of good quality mustang mares they had caught and described the buckskin stallion. He also explained how the Indian had gentled down the stallion the Indian way and how he had the stallion saddle broken so much faster and how amazed he and his cowboys were. He also explained how they used the same method to saddle break the geldings they had added to their horse cavvy so they'd have plenty of riding stock for the trip north.

"So you're headed up to Kansas again?" she asked. She already knew that was what he had planned.

"Yes," he answered.

"With a herd of cattle?"

"Almost three thousand head," was his answer.

When they went to the Allen residence at the end of the day, Scamp was jumping up and down and scampering around, obviously glad to see them.

"I want you to teach Scamp some new tricks," Vickie said.

"I can do that," answered Jim.

Vickie went inside to see if her mother needed any help with supper. Jim stayed outside and worked with Scamp. Vickie had already taught him to stay and to come when called. So Jim just had him practice sitting, standing, lying down, and getting up. Then he had him practice staying and coming when called. That was just a review of what the puppy had already learned. So Jim taught him to roll over on command. That was a new trick.

They played music that night as usual.

The next morning, Jim saddled up his gray right after breakfast to ride back out and join the herd. For some reason, Vickie didn't feel the heavy loss of his leaving like she always had before. Jim had proposed to her the last time he had seen her. She had already set a wedding date. She told him to make sure he got back by November 15. It was the first week of September by now. Jim figured he had plenty of time.

After Jim rejoined the herd, Ben told him he wanted to take off a couple of days. Jill's farm was only half a day's ride ahead. Jim told him fine.

Ben rode up to Jill's farm to find her hoeing her garden. Little Jacob had a smaller hoe and was attempting to help her. He'd chop at the tough weeds without much luck. Jill had encouraged him to cut the smaller weeds, but he wanted to attack the big, tough weeds like she was doing. When she saw Ben, she squealed and ran to him, tossing down her hoe. Little Jacob did the same. By the time he had dismounted, both of them were hugging him.

"Are you staying for dinner?" she asked.

"Do you think I'd miss out on a chance to eat your cooking?" he said.

So Jill decided to leave off hoeing and start cooking something for her two men to eat. Ben walked over and looked at her goat pasture before he walked over to the cabin. Little Jacob tagged long. The calves were really growing. Most of them were bigger than their surrogate mothers by now. He still thought the method she had decided to use to get a herd of cattle to raise was neat—have a herd of goat nannies raise a bunch of orphan calves.

Then Ben led his horse over to the corral, put him inside, and unsaddled him. Jacob just stood and watched him. He hung the saddle and bridle on the corral fence. His horse lay down and rolled before doing anything else. Then he went over to the water trough and drank. Ben went to the pump and pumped the trough full of water again. He wanted him to still have more water if he wanted to drink again later. But he also wanted to keep Jill's water trough full for the nanny goats and calves. She had a creek running through her big pasture, but this was the only place they had water in her small pasture. The corral fence was built so that the watering trough went under it, so that half the trough was inside the corral and the other half outside so the goats and calves in the pasture could come up and drink. After that, he went to the barn, climbed up into the loft, and forked down some hay.

After an excellent meal of goat stew, Ben went out and found another hoe and started hoeing the garden with Jill and Jacob. A cowboy normally didn't like to work off the back of a horse if he could get out of it. It never occurred to Ben; he wanted Jill's garden hoed too.

And the three of them working together had it done by midafternoon.

CHAPTER 36

Stampedes

On their first night on the trail, thunder and lightning started playing shortly after dark. The herd was up and running almost instantly. All the cowboys were out of their blankets and mounted on their night horses immediately. The cattle ran all night long. It was sunup before they got them to milling and a couple of hours after that before the chuck wagon caught up. The men didn't get breakfast until mid-morning. The cattle finally settled down to graze. All that running must have given them an appetite.

It definitely gave the men an appetite. They were starving by the time they could finally eat. The teenage boys endured the loss of sleep better than the grown men but seemed to not endure the hunger as well. They were worn out from riding all night, but nervous energy kept them going. And they were starving—even more than the adult cowboys. Every man in the crew had two helpings of breakfast that morning—biscuits and gravy and bacon. And everyone drank more coffee than usual.

They kept the herd on their feet until nightfall. Then they finally let them bed down. But they had no more than bedded down and settled when they were on their feet and running again. There was no thunder or lightning this time. Jim was trying to figure out the reason why they wanted to run again when they hadn't even had any sleep in thirty-six hours.

They ran till morning again, but they got them milling at about sunup. The boys were starving at the breakfast fire again and ate with a hearty appetite. The steers wanted to bed down, but Jim wasn't going to have any of that. If they weren't going to graze, then they'd just get them moving up the trail. It took a lot of swearing and yelling to get them going. Finally, in the middle of the afternoon, the cattle acted like they wanted to graze, so Jim told Ben to let them stop and fill their bellies.

But the steers were no more than bedded down and seeming like they were settled for the night before they stampeded again. The cowboys began to wonder if they were ever going to get any sleep.

The following night, the herd bedded down and slept till morning. So Jim guessed there was a limit to the endurance of even an ornery longhorn steer. The men still had to take their turn at night guard, so they didn't catch up on their sleep; but at least they all got a few hours of sleep. When they came to the fire for breakfast that morning, everyone was bleary-eyed and didn't move overly fast.

Three nights later, they stampeded again. They still couldn't get them milling until morning. And Jim couldn't figure out any reason for it. He was sitting his horse that night near the chuck wagon when an old cowboy that Jim had hired at Waco rode up to him.

"There's one steer in the herd that's causing all the stampedes."

"Tell me more about that," Jim said.

The cowboy, named Rocky, said, "If you'll come and ride around the herd with me, I'll show you." So he wheeled his horse and followed Rocky as they rode along parallel to the herd. There was a full moon, so they could see the cattle well enough after they had bedded down.

Jim started singing as always to keep the cattle from spooking at the sight of riders. After they had ridden about halfway around the herd, Rocky pointed to a black steer with white spots on his back and one horn twisted around to the front of his head. He said, "That's him."

So Jim rode back to the fire and gave orders to two of the men to rope the black-and-white steer with the twisted horn and pull him out of the herd and shoot him. He told them where to find him. Both cowboys had to get a rope on him to pull him out of the herd. The disturbance caused the herd to instantly come to their feet.

But they didn't run this time. They were still pretty tired from their exertions of the past week. The two cowboys got the black-and-white steer clear of the herd, and he started running. The two cowboys just spurred their horses and kept him running till he was well clear of the herd. They heard a shot ring out in the distance.

Jim rode out toward the direction he had heard the shot, and he came up to the two cowboys. He said, "Let's butcher the steer. We're getting low on meat anyway." So they rode back out to the steer, skinned it out, field dressed it, and quartered the meat. There was enough moonlight that they could see how to work. They divided up the meat and tied it behind their saddles and took it to the chuck wagon. So now they should have enough meat to last them a few weeks.

The herd never stampeded again all the way to Abilene with only one exception. And that was in an Indian fight. After they got into Indian country, they had a brush with Indians as usual, but since they were ready for them, they fought them off without losing any stock.

*****

They reached Kansas with the herd of 2,923 steers that sold for $23 a head for a total of $67,229. Jim had never had so much money in his life! He sold the horses he didn't want to bring back with him for $40 a head. There were forty-two horses he decided he could spare, so that was another $1,680. That made his gross income $68,909. After he paid the hands and bought the supplies he needed for the return trip, he still had $67,516. So he headed back to Texas with enough money to operate his new ranch for a couple of years. And he would need that long before he'd have any cattle of his own to make a drive with. He figured he could buy cattle again the following summer and make a drive or two anyway. It looked like he was finally making his start.

CHAPTER 37

Squatters

When they reached the ranch, smoke was coming from the chimney of the bunkhouse. That looked normal enough. But then he saw strange horses in the corral. That didn't look so normal.

Jim left the chuck wagon and horse cavvy with two men to guard it and led the other six men up to the cookshack cautiously. "Hello," Jim called.

A man in an apron stuck his head out the door. He was a stranger.

"What are you doing here?" Jim asked.

"I'm the cook," he replied.

"But I didn't hire you," Jim returned.

"This is a line camp for the Bar OB spread," he answered. "The Bar OB hired me."

"This is the Slant JB spread," Jim then said.

"The owner of the Bar OB found it abandoned and set up a line camp here."

Jim immediately wondered what happened to the three men he had left to watch the place!

But he only asked, "Where's the foreman of the Bar OB?"

"Out riding somewhere, looking for strays to be branded."

Jim then took his men and rode out into the horse pasture. After riding all over the horse pasture, he didn't find his herd of brood-mares or the buckskin stallion anywhere. He saw a herd of strange horses and a herd of broodmares with colts with a strange stallion out grazing with them.

Jim took his crew of cowboys and left the ranch. He wanted to find his horse herd, first of all. And he wanted to find out what happened to the three cowboys he had left behind to guard the ranch and He Who Flies.

Jim and the six cowboys rode back to the chuck wagon and horse cavvy. He explained to the cook and the two horse guards what was going on. Then Jim led the chuck wagon and horse herd to a place that would be more easily defended. He left them there to make camp and then started riding a circle around the ranch, looking for the missing men and horses. He brought his six cowboys along with him. Ben was among them.

He decided to check the east side of the ranch first since the Bar OB spread was on the west side. He and his crew of searchers rode north first, with no sign of the missing men or stock. The ranch headquarters was on the south side of the horse pasture, so when he didn't find them, he just swung farther east, turned south, and continued his search. They were getting closer to Jack's spread.

He saw the herd of broodmares first with the buckskin stallion grazing nearby. Then he saw the smoke from a campfire and rode that direction. He found the three missing men.

He had left Adam in charge of the other two men when he left them there to guard the ranch. He rode up to the fire and called out, "Hello, the fire. It's Jim."

"Why, hello," Adam called back.

Jim and his cowboys dismounted. Jim shook hands with Adam. One of the cowboys was out loose herding the herd of mares. Adam had a big pot of coffee on the fire. So each cowboy got a cup of coffee and rolled a smoke.

"So can you tell me what happened?" Jim then asked.

"Yes. The Bar OB crew attacked us without warning," said Adam. "We were outnumbered three to one, so I decided to save the horse herd. We got the herd of broodmares clear and brought them out here. Bar OB riders came out three times and tried to steal the herd of broodmares from us, but we fought them off each time." Jim saw a bandage on Alvin's arm.

"Can you tell me where He Who Flies is at?" Jim then asked.

"Yes. He's been scouting around. He comes in and takes a turn at wrangling the horses every day or two but doesn't stay here."

"Well, let's take the horses up to the chuck wagon," Jim told him. So Adam poured the remains of the coffee on the fire to put it out and mounted up. Jim and the cowboys got the horse herd moving in the direction where they had left the chuck wagon.

It was near evening when they came up to the chuck wagon. He saw He Who Flies was out with the horses and the other two had started supper. The chuck wagon cook fixed a meal for the crew and Jim explained to them that they would retake the Slant JB Ranch the following morning. He decided to wait until midmorning when the Bar OB riders had ridden out to look for strays.

Jim had the cook move the chuck wagon up closer to the ranch and had them bring the horse herd closer as well. Then Jim left the cook and four men to guard the chuck wagon and horse herd. At about midmorning, he took the other seven men and approached the Slant JB ranch from the north. He had the men remove the rails of the fence for about thirty yards or so. Then they simply rode around the Bar OB horse herd and drove them out of the pasture. Jim then checked the bunkhouse and made sure no one was there. Then he took two men and rode to the cookshack and put a gun on the cook. Then he sent a man to go let the men who were guarding Slant JB horses know to drive the horses into the horse pasture. They then put the rails back up. Jim let the Bar OB cook saddle one of the horses in the corral, then they drove the rest of the horses out and made them scatter in the direction of the Bar OB range.

Jim and his men kept watch all day, expecting an attack from the Bar OB riders, but it didn't come. They must have seen the cook leaving and learned from him what happened. For the next week, Jim had two men guarding the horse herd inside the pasture night and day and the rest of the men patrolling the perimeter of the ranch in case the Bar OB crew should attack again. All was quiet for a week. Jim decided to relax his guard and resume branding mavericks. They operated from ranch headquarters since they were finding cattle to brand near the ranch.

Then they were attacked at breakfast. The attackers attempted to open the gate to the corral to let their horses loose. Jim was watching from the window and shot the man trying to open the corral gate. The men inside the bunkhouse grabbed their six-guns and started shooting too. Several of the men had kept their rifles in the bunkhouse and started firing out the windows. Jim's rifle was in the cabin. Ben shot one of the squatters out of his saddle as he rode by firing at them. Two of the outlaws had headed for the horse herd to stampede them. Ben leveled down at them through a back window and shot both of them out of the saddle. The horse herd was spooked from all the shooting and ran to the northern end of the horse pasture. The rails of the fence had been removed, so the horse herd left the pasture, but with the men who tried to steal them dead, they ran in no particular direction.

After the shooting was over, four of the outlaws lay dead, and the horse herd was gone. Jim decided to retrieve the horses first. So he left half the men behind to keep guard on the ranch, and he and five men rode after the horse herd. They overcame them about ten miles north of the ranch and turned them and drove them back into the pasture. They put the rails to the fence back up and then rode back to the ranch headquarters. They tied the four dead bodies on their horses and turned them loose. They knew the horses would go home.

After a few days, when things seemed to return to normal, Jim decided they probably wouldn't attack again. So he went to town to find builders to hire to build a ranch house. He knew the cabin wouldn't be adequate for his new bride.

CHAPTER 38

Land Grabbers and Sleepers

The Bar OB riders rode up to the Harper farm. Nesters! They'd get rid of them in short order. It was midmorning when they rode into the yard. They saw a house, a rail fence, a long log building, and some hogpens. There was another log house that they didn't know what it was for.

Beyond that was a cornfield. A man, three boys, and two girls were out hoeing the corn. "Hello," Bo said. The man looked up. "This is Bar OB range. You'll have to leave." The three boys and the two girls disappeared in the cornfield. It was waist-high.

"I homesteaded this land. It's legally mine," the man told him.

"Well, you homesteaded some land on the Bar OB range, and you can't stay."

"We'll stay," Ollie told them.

Bo raised his rifle as did his men and leveled it at him. "You'll leave. You have until sundown to be gone."

Three boys appeared on the roof of the chicken house with rifles pointed at the land grabbers. "We'll stay," Ollie repeated.

Bo looked at the rifles then looked again at the old man. There had to be a reason why he was so calm, and he now saw that reason.

"We'll come back with more men. Make sure you're gone by morning," Bo then said.

"Bring all the men you want. We'll be here," Ollie said.

Bo and his men rode off. This wasn't as easy as he thought it would be!

187

Bo was back again at the crack of dawn the next morning. This time, he brought a dozen men with him. He rode up to the cabin and called out. No one answered. Bo looked around. There appeared to be no one there! There weren't any horses in the corral. Maybe they did pack up and leave. He rode a little to the right, where there was a hogpen, and looked over the fence. There were still hogs there.

He dismounted and walked up to the cabin. He stepped up to the doorstep and started to open the door. A shot rang out, and a bullet ricocheted off the doorframe. He jumped back and drew his six-gun. He looked around but didn't see anybody! Then gunfire erupted everywhere, hitting the ground near the horse's hooves. The horses spooked and started running in spite of the riders trying to control them. Bo's horse ran off too, leaving him standing there.

Then a man and three boys appeared out of the woods facing the cabin with rifles leveled at Bo. They came within about twenty feet of him and then stopped.

"You're trespassing," Ollie told him. Bo just stared at him flabbergasted. Ollie paused a minute and then said, "Take your boots off." Bo did nothing. So two boys shoved him down and yanked his boots off. Then Ollie said, "Now get up." Bo couldn't think of anything else to do, so he got up. "Now start walking." Ollie and his boys kept their rifles leveled at him until he walked out of sight.

There was a pasture to the south of the cornfield where two milk cows were grazing. One of the boys went and walked behind them and started driving them up to the barn. It was time to do the milking and feeding the hogs and chickens and gathering up the eggs. Then Becky would harness up the team and start her trip to one of the ranches nearby to sell them.

*****

After Jim decided that the Bar OB crew wasn't going to try to steal his ranch again, he and the men set out to ride the range outside the horse pasture and check on the Slant JB cattle. They knew they had more calves to brand. Jim rode with the branding crew, and they used the chuck wagon so they could camp wherever they managed to round up a herd of cattle that had calves that needed branding.

It was still warm in the mornings when they rolled out of their blankets and went to the chuck wagon to get chuck. Jim was normally the first one up, with the exception of the cook and the cook's helper of course. So he had gone to the fire and poured himself a cup of coffee and then sat on a rock, sipping coffee while he watched the gray of dawn in the east gradually grow brighter. When the cook yelled, "Come and get it!" he went and got a plate of biscuits and gravy and bacon and then ate. Then he went to the rope corral and roped a bronc and saddled up. He saddled one of the roans this time. He wanted to give the newly broke broncs all the experience under the saddle he could, and riding circle was a good way to do it.

There was a lot of motion in the rope corral as each man went and saddled a horse to start the morning's work. Jim picked a circle going to the west of the chuck wagon. It was daylight by now. So he looked for calves that hadn't been earmarked. That meant they hadn't been branded yet. Jim rode by several cows with big calves that had already been earmarked. It was an accident that he happened to ride by a calf and see the left side. There was no brand on it. Now that wasn't right! If it had an earmark, it should have a brand! They always earmarked a calf when they branded it so they wouldn't have to ride all the way around it to see if it had a brand when looking for unbranded stock.

So Jim started riding all the way around each calf and looking to see if it had a brand even if it was already earmarked. He found that four out of five of the earmarked calves had not been branded! Sleepered stock!

So he started gathering up the sleepered calves with their mothers and put them in the bunch of the unbranded calves he was gathering. He reached the chuck wagon with his gather and hazed them into the herd of cattle to be branded and unsaddled and turned his horse loose in the rope corral.

He walked over to the fire after the men were all there and got their plates filled with food and their coffee cups filled.

He told them, "I found some sleepered stock this morning."

He had their attention then. This was something no one expected.

"So riding circle is going to take longer than usual because you have to ride all the way around each calf to see if it has a brand. You can't pay any attention to earmarks."

He knew he still needed to find out who was sleepering his calves, but they could handle that later. For now, they knew they needed to do their fall branding.

After chuck, they went out to the herd and got a branding fire going and started their work of branding the maverick calves. They had worked all morning getting a herd of cattle together to be branded, and then they spent the afternoon branding. They were tired when the day was finally done.

Rustlers

Solving the problem with the sleepered calves caused the branding to take more time, but it nullified the effect of the rustlers' sleepering the calves to begin with. Jim had thought the problem of rustling was solved. But after several weeks, Jim noticed that they still didn't see near as many Slant JB cattle as they had before they left for the drive to Kansas. And they saw a lot more Bar BB cattle. And almost all of them were freshly branded.

They needed fresh meat for the bunkhouse anyway, and so Jim told one of the men to shoot a Bar BB calf and skin it. Then he had a couple of other men cut up and quarter the meat while he examined the hide. Sure enough, it had been altered from the Slant JB to the Bar BB!

So the Bar BB had been busy rustling Slant JB stock the entire time that they were gone! There were still mavericks to brand, but they continued to see more Bar BB cattle and less Slant JB cattle as they went along.

Jim had the men ride circle in pairs and told them that if they saw any indications of trouble, to ride back to the chuck wagon and report it to him before doing anything. In the meantime, Jim took two cowboys with him and just rode ahead and scouted the area ahead of the roundup crew to see what was going on.

Jim saw a plume of smoke just over a rise. He rode up carefully, and as soon as he topped the rise, he saw two men with a calf down and hogtied with a branding iron. The calf had a Slant JB brand,

and a man was working on the brand with a running iron, obviously changing it to a Bar BB.

Jim undid the strap on his six-gun and rode up to them. The man holding the branding iron saw him, dropped the branding iron, and grabbed for his gun. The man holding the calf's head jumped up and did likewise. Jim pulled his gun and shot them both before they could clear leather.

The cow had been thrown and hog-tied, too, to keep her from interfering. Jim dismounted and approached the fire carefully. Both the rustlers were dead. He turned the calf loose first, then the cow. They scampered off.

So Jim decided that he and his men had better just start a massive search for rustlers. They discontinued the branding and started riding the range west of the ranch looking for any sign of anything that shouldn't be going on.

Jim had the men spread out but told them not to start a fight if they saw rustlers but to ride back to the chuck wagon and wait for the rest of the men to arrive. He also had them ride in pairs.

Jim rode in a large circle and arrived back at the chuck wagon at noon. He had Zeke ride with him. They had not seen any sign of rustlers. They unsaddled their horses and turned them into the rope corral. Just wrangling the horses was still Mark's job.

"I'd like to help look for rustlers," Mark said when he got a plate of chuck and sat down on a rock at the fire.

"Your job is to keep the rustlers from stealing the horses. Without them, we'd be in big trouble," Jim told him. And Jim noticed he didn't have a belt gun. He went to his saddlebags and got one of his spare six-guns and brought it to him. It was the one with a holster, and he also brought along a spare cylinder that was loaded. Then he got out his pouch of bullets and sack of primers. It was a gun that shot loose ammunition.

"Here, fasten this to your belt," he told Mark. "Do you know how to work it?"

"No, I've always used my rifle." Now a muzzle-loading rifle isn't very good up against men with repeating rifles.

Jim showed Mark how to change out a cylinder when it went empty. And he explained how to just cock it, point it, and fire it. "You can get by on this for now," Jim said. "When it goes empty, change to the other cylinder. Your powder from your powder horn will work when you have to reload your cylinders, but you'll have to use the bullets from this bullet pouch." He showed him the small leather bag loaded with bullets. "These are .45-caliber bullets. Your rifle shoots .54-caliber bullets, so you'll have to have a different pouch of bullets for the six-gun. There is also a ramrod in the bullet pouch to seat the bullet after loading a chamber with powder. And you'll have to prime each chamber on the cylinder." He took one primer out and put it back in to show him how to do that. "Put the bullet pouch in one of your vest pockets and the sack of primers in another." So his wrangler now at least had a six-gun.

Mark still carried his Hawkins rifle over his saddle horn when he let the horses out of the rope corral after each man saddled a new horse. But he had a belt gun now. He wouldn't have time to reload the Hawkins in a fight. It was good for one shot only.

The men resumed riding their large circles looking for any sign of rustling. After two days of searching, they saw no further sign of them. So Jim concluded that the rustlers were wise to the fact they were looking for them. He then decided to just resume branding for now.

They still saw a lot of sleepered stock and brought them in and branded them. And they kept seeing a lot of freshly branded Bar BB cattle that Jim suspected had brands that had been altered. But Jim still knew that the more mavericks that were branded with the Slant JB brand, the better off he would be.

Then Jim thought of an idea. What would he do if he was a rustler? He'd work the areas where the Slant JB crew had already been, not the direction that they were going. So one morning, he moved the chuck wagon back in the direction where they had already covered the area and started riding circles in pairs to see what they found. At noon, when they met at the chuck wagon for dinner, Ben reported that he saw a gathering of a herd of cattle about five miles or so from the chuck wagon to the southwest. So Jim had all the men ride with him to the area. Sure enough, they found the herd of cattle and half a dozen men—two of them keeping the herd bunched up, two of them roping cattle and bringing them to the branding fire, and two of them altering Slant JB brands to Bar BB. When they saw Jim and his riders, the man holding the branding iron immediately dropped the iron and grabbed for his gun. Jim drew his six-gun and shot him.

The rustlers ran to the nearby rocks and opened fire. Jim and his men had to scatter to avoid their gunfire. They dismounted and found positions in the rocks too so they could return their fire. The cattle, no longer herded, scattered. And Jim recognized Jeb and Gene running toward the rocks with the other rustlers! So they were rustling Slant JB stock too!

Jim had managed to find a spot where he could tie his horse to a bush and get the rifle out of his saddle boot. He preferred a rifle when he had the choice. He used his six-gun when he didn't have time to get out his rifle.

Jim heard a gunshot and saw a puff of smoke from behind a rock and fired at the puff of smoke. He heard a yell, and the gun clattered as it fell among the rocks. Firing was going on all around him. The melee sounded just like the battles that took place during the war that Jim was all too familiar with. Most of the men in Jim's crew were veterans of the war. So he knew this would be old hat to them. The teenagers in the outfit would have been too young to go to war.

Jim kept firing at each puff of smoke that he saw, then he heard a yell from Al, the man to his right. He dropped his gun and fell, holding his shoulder. Jim laid down his rifle to check on him. A bullet had gone through his shoulder. He crawled back to his horse and, standing up on the far side of him, got some bandages out of his saddlebags. Then he got down and crawled back to where Al lay. He took out his hunting knife and cut his clothing away from the wound, then put a fistful of bandages against it to staunch the blood flow. After a few minutes, the bleeding stopped, and he finished bandaging the wound. Another man yelled and fell nearby, obviously dead.

Jim knew if he was going to win this battle, he'd have to use better tactics than this. And what would be the likeliest tactic? The ground was lower behind the rocks. So Jim motioned to each man he could see to get back. Then he crawled around among the rocks so he could let each man know what he planned. The firing stopped as Jim and his men gathered behind the rocks. There was no longer anything to shoot at. Then Jim briefed them on what to do.

So Jim and his men mounted their horses, rode to the lower ground where the rustlers couldn't see them, then maneuvered around to the right. Then they rushed the rustlers from horseback from the right flank, which would, of course, be the rustlers' left flank. They heard bullets strike flesh and yells when men were hit. Almost immediately, the rustlers dropped their guns and held up their hands—three of them. Three of Jim's men dismounted, pulled a piece of piggin' string out their pockets, where they always kept it, and went up and tied their hands. Jeb and Gene were included in the three. Three of the rustlers were already dead. They took the three that were still alive with their hands tied behind their backs, had them mount their horses, and led them down to the creek where there was a big enough cottonwood tree. Three of the men rigged their lariat ropes with a hangman's noose and tossed their rope over a limb of the tree. There was one limb on the tree that was long enough for all three.

Hanging the three surviving rustlers only took a few minutes. He saw Jeb and Gene kick when their horses were whipped from underneath them. They rode away, leaving them dangling from the cottonwood tree.

Well, he'd have no more trouble from Jeb and Gene now.

A Spark of Romance

Becky maneuvered her buckboard toward where she thought maybe the Rolling J chuck wagon might be. She expected they'd be working the northern part of their range by now. She saw a herd of horses that was apparently being herded by a teenage boy. She headed over in his direction. When she got close enough, she said, "Hello. My name is Becky."

Mark looked over and said, "My name is Mark."

"I'm looking for the chuck wagon," Becky then said.

"It'll be along in a little bit. We're moving our camp. I'm letting the horses graze so they'll be ready when the cowboys need fresh mounts at noon."

"All right. I brought some eggs."

"Well, that's good. We've been having eggs every morning or so since you started coming by." The cowboys all appreciated fresh eggs but rarely got them except when they went into town. So the sight of Becky's buckboard was always welcome.

Becky was a beautiful girl to begin with, but Mark noticed she looked especially pretty today. "Where should I park my buckboard?" she then asked.

"Probably in that clearing next to the creek over there. But don't park it over on the right there. That's where the chuck wagon will park, and there's room for a rope corral on the other side of it." So Becky moved her buckboard over to the left side of the clearing, set the brake, and got down. Mark got a glimpse of a work boot at the hem of her dress when she stepped down. So she apparently wore work boots just like a man did, but she had on a long full dress as was the custom for ladies.

Mark just sat his horse watching the horses graze. Becky walked out to him and said, "Where are you from?"

"Over to the west of here. We had a farm, but it got burned out by Indians."

"Oh! I didn't know." She didn't ask what happened to his parents. She figured he'd tell her if he wanted her to know.

"How about you?" Mark asked.

"We came from Tennessee. Pa decided to come out West and raise chickens and hogs. He knew that cowboys liked bacon but also that they liked eggs. And they normally didn't get eggs because they wouldn't keep at a chuck wagon or bunkhouse."

"Yeah, I wonder why nobody thought of that before. A rancher would be laughed at if he kept chickens or hogs either one."

"But they don't laugh at us because we're farmers."

Mark knew they didn't laugh, but there were lots of ranchers that would try to run them off if they started a farm on their range.

"We started our farm before there were very many ranchers here. It took us a year to grow a crop to get feed for our livestock. Then we bought the chickens and some sow pigs. Now we have a pen full of hogs and a chicken yard full of chickens."

"I wonder why you don't let your hogs run out like most farmers do around here," Mark then said.

"Pa said they'd run weight off if we did. We keep them in a pen and feed them corn. We have a big granary that Pa and the boys built the first year we were here. That's when they built the hogpens and chicken house too. They built the cabin first so we'd have a place to live, but after they planted the crop that first year, any extra time we had was spent on building sheds, chicken houses, and such. And the barn. We have to have that for the milk cows.

"We mainly lived off the wild game the boys shot that first year. We brought several hundred-pound sacks of potatoes and beans when we first moved here. And a barrel of flour. That was what we lived on, but we had only wild meat."

"We lived off wild meat mostly," Mark said. "Deer meat and sometimes squirrels or rabbits."

They saw the chuck wagon come rolling over the rise to the south. So it would be setting up, and the cooks would start cooking dinner. Becky waited until the cook and the cook's flunky got the fire built and grub cooked before she went over and asked the cook if he needed any eggs. The cook bought all she had of course. He also bought a side of bacon from her. Since it was nearly noon, the cook asked her if she'd like to eat with them.

So Becky sat down on a log and had dinner with twelve hungry cowboys.

*****

Jim knew he had to stop the rustling. But he also knew he had to find out who was really doing it. He decided to pay a social call on the Bar OB ranch.

He took three cowboys along, but when he approached the OB ranch buildings, he told them to stay out of sight and ride up only in the event of trouble. He boldly rode into the yard and hailed the house. It was almost noon by then. A man came out of the bunk-house with his hand near his gun and asked him to state his business.

"I'm here to see Oscar Brown," Jim knew that was the name of the Bar OB owner.

"He's not seeing anyone," the man replied.

"I'll hear it from him," Jim answered. Then he said, "And who are you?"

"I'm the Bar OB foreman, and I know the boss ain't seeing anyone."

"What's going on out here?" a voice called from the doorstep of the ranch house.

"I'm Jim Bennett, and I've come to get acquainted," Jim called.

"Why, come in, come in. We're neighbors. I tried to pay a call on you a month or so ago, and you were gone. They said you were taking a herd of steers up the trail. I'd do the same if I were younger. Come on in and set. The cook nearly has dinner ready."

So Jim found himself setting at the dinner table having an excellent meal of beefsteak, potatoes, biscuits, and gravy with a steaming cup of coffee in his hand. Oscar Brown looked to be past fifty and had thinning hair and a paunch around his middle. But he apparently enjoyed talking and was glad of the opportunity to get acquainted with his neighbor.

During the course of the conversation, Jim decided that this man was not a rustler. He could just tell. He was too open, too frank, and too friendly. Then Jim remembered the men he had left hidden near the ranch. They hadn't eaten. After dinner was over, he excused himself and went out. The Bar OB men had all finished eating and had gone to the corral to each rope a fresh horse to resume their work. Jim just walked over to the cookshack and asked the cook if there was any grub left. The cook told him, "No. The men ate it all." Jim recognized the cook as the one that had been squatting on his land that he and his men had run off.

Jim walked on into the kitchen and started lifting up lids and such. There was almost half a pot of stew left and plenty of coffee left in the pot. He saw almost a full pan of biscuits sitting on the stove. Jim stepped out on the doorstep and put his thumb and finger in his mouth and let out a whistle. He faced the cook as if to say, "What are you going to do about it?" The cook had an intimidated look on his face. Jim's three men rode into the yard, and Jim told them to tie their horses to the hitching rail and come on in. He stood there while the cook dished them out some stew, biscuits, and coffee.

After they had eaten and ridden off, Jim said, "The old man doesn't know any rustling is going on. There's something that doesn't meet the eye here."

"Really?" said Zeke. "That is interesting."

They continued their ride and saw some calves that had been branded with the Slant JB brand. The brands were fresh, except the brands were more smeared than they should be. He kept on seeing the smeared Slant JB brands on calves as they rode on back to their ranch. When they were near the Slant JB ranch, Jim had one of the men rope a weaned calf showing one of those smeared Slant JB brands. They took it up near the cookshack, shot it, and started skinning it out. When Jim looked at the inside of the hide, he could tell it had been changed from Bar OB to Slant JB.

So Jim started to put two and two together. He had decided that the rancher himself was honest. He might not have even known that his foreman and some of his men had tried to squat on his land. And he was sure he didn't know about any rustling going on. So who would benefit from a fight between the Bar OB and the Slant JB? He'd have to think on that some more, but the Bar OB foreman tried to keep him from seeing the rancher. That made the foreman himself a prime suspect.

Jim rode to town to check and see just what names the Bar OB and Bar BB were registered under. He found out that the Bar OB was registered under the rancher's name, Oscar Brown. But the Bar BB was registered under the Bar OB *foreman's* name, Buster Beckett. If there was a fight between the Slant JB and the Bar OB and they killed each other off, the foreman with the Bar BB brand could take over both ranches!

The next morning, Jim and five men rode out to the Bar OB ranch. They timed it to get there early enough so that the rancher would still be there. They had brought along the two hides, one that showed the brand altered from Slant JB to Bar OB and the other that had been altered from a Bar OB to Slant JB. The rancher came out. Jim showed him both hides.

"Looks like someone wants us to fight each other. If we killed each other off, he could take over both ranches," Jim said.

Oscar Brown immediately saw what was going on. He called out Buster Beckett and showed him the two hides. He told him he was fired. Then he fired everyone loyal to him so they could have peace on the range again.

CHAPTER 41

Mark Goes Courtin'

It was Saturday night, and the men all got paid. They were in the bunkhouse getting a shave and bath in preparation for going to town. They heated up water on the stove, and several cowboys got a bath in the same bathwater. When it started getting too dirty, two cowboys would take the tub out and empty it, and they'd heat more water. Mark got his turn at taking a bath too. And he decided to shave. All he had on his face was peach fuzz, but he didn't want peach fuzz on his face. He had asked Becky if he could come calling the last time she came by to deliver eggs, and she had said yes. So he wanted to look his best.

So after he shaved and had a bath, he put on his best shirt and then went out and saddled up. The other cowboys were saddling up too. Mark rode his horse to the northwest, where he thought the Harper farm would be. He just kept on riding. He headed toward the creek. When he reached it, he just followed the creek on north. He came to a rail fence and a cornfield. Then he saw the buildings. They had a chicken house, a barn, a cabin, and a corral.

He rode up to the yard and yelled, "Hello, the house!" The door opened.

Someone said, "Come in."

Mark tied his horse to the hitch rail and walked up the steps and through the door. "Hello, Mark!" Becky said when she saw him. She was helping her Ma put food on the table. Her two sisters were helping too.

"Hello," Mark mumbled. He didn't really know what to say.

"Pull up a chair and set," Pa told him. He had a friendly ring to his voice. He had decided he liked Mark the instant he walked in the door. He hadn't seen him before. Becky had seen all the Rolling J punchers, of course, and got acquainted with several of them.

"I need to go take care of my horse," Mark said.

"Sure," Pa answered. "You can go put him in the corral."

So Mark went out, put his horse in the corral, and unsaddled him. When he came back in, Pa said, "Pull up a chair." The girls had finished putting food on the table, so they sat down too. Pa said the blessing, then they started eating. Then Mark noticed the food—pork ribs, baked potatoes, biscuits, homemade butter. And jam! It looked like peach jam. After Mark started eating, he figured out the Harper women definitely knew how to cook. He hadn't eaten grub cooked by a woman in a long time.

"Where did you learn to shoot a rifle?" asked Conn. He was the oldest boy in the family. He was nineteen.

"At our farm over west of here," answered Mark. "We needed deer meat."

"I see you pack a six-gun too," Walt remarked. Walt was the second oldest boy. He was seventeen.

"Had to. We've had problems with rustlers." Mark didn't mention that he hadn't really learned how to shoot it yet. There was no time to even practice. But he kept it on his hip in case he did need it. It never dawned on him that it might be better to not pack a gun unless you know how to use it.

"Why does everyone keep talking about guns?" Joanne asked. She was thirteen. Becky was fifteen. Sally was the youngest kid in the family. She was eleven.

Hubert was fourteen. He had peach fuzz on his face too, just like Mark did before he had shaved. He didn't think about shaving it off like Mark did. He had been quiet so far. He couldn't think of anything to say.

After they finished the meal, Becky got up and brought a peach pie to the table. She cut it and dished out a piece for eight people. She served Mark first. Then she went to the counter across the kitchen and got another pie and cut a piece for herself. So she was making it obvious that folks could have seconds if they wanted it.

"Got our own peach tree," Ollie mumbled as he took a bite out of his pie.

Mark still felt ill at ease. He wasn't accustomed to being around a whole family of strangers. And Becky had said very little during the meal. She couldn't think of anything to say either. Mark felt all stiff inside. They were all strangers, except Becky, and she was being very quiet. Finally, to break the silence, Sally, the youngest girl said, "Do you ever ride bucking horses?"

"I have, but normally, I don't. I'm the horse wrangler. I herd the horses and bring them in to the chuck wagon when the cowboys need to change to a fresh horse."

"Sounds exciting," Sally said.

"I see you're raising corn," Mark finally said. "We raised corn on our farm."

"We feed the corn to our hogs and chickens," Conn said. He seemed completely at ease, which helped ease Mark's tension a little.

"We raised hogs and chickens too," Mark said. "And we had two milk cows. I usually went to the nearby woods and shot a deer when we needed meat. But we raised most of our grub in our garden."

"Yeah, we have a big garden too," Conn said. "That's where the beans and okra came from."

"What do you plan to do in the future?" Becky then asked. Mark's conversation with Conn sort of helped her come out of her shell a little.

"I'm planning to change over to a regular cowboy's job if they hire someone younger than me," he replied. "But I'm also thinking I might start my own farm someday. I like being a cowboy okay, but I liked farming too."

"You could homestead some land," Ollie then said. "If you started a homestead near here, we'd be neighbors." Becky brightened up a little at that. She hadn't thought of the possibility of Mark being their neighbor.

"I could do that. I'd have to save up the money to buy a couple of plow horses and a plow. I could just build a barn, a corral, and a cabin. And I could build a rail fence around it too so that the cattle that roam the free range wouldn't eat my crops."

"And you could raise hogs and chickens, and I could sell eggs for you," Becky then piped up.

"Yeah," Mark reflected. "But for now, I need a job and I have a job. It will take a while to save enough to buy a team of horses and a plow just from my wages. And I'd need to buy an ax and crosscut saw too."

After supper, Sally brought Pa a fiddle. Pa tuned it and started playing. It was a fast hoedown tune. Sally and Joanne got on the floor and started dancing. They did a jig dance. Mom and Becky did the dishes.

After a few tunes, Mark got up and started doing a jig. The music just made you feel like dancing. After a few more songs, Becky came and stood in front of him and started dancing too. She had a beautiful smile on her face. It seemed like the music brought her and Mark both out of their shells.

When it started getting late, Mark went out and saddled his horse and started back to Jim's ranch. He had really enjoyed the evening and hated to leave, but he needed to get back.

Horse Rancher

Jim rode out to his horse pasture and rode around his horse herd. The stallion whinnied when he saw him. He was still overcome with the beauty of the big stallion every time he saw him. He had big shoulders and a big neck, and his mane was long and flowing. He had a black streak down his back and a black tail as was usual with buckskins. His mane wasn't black but was buckskin-colored like the rest of his body except for a black forelock. His hair had a nice sheen to it from grazing the green grass.

Jim's idea when he first decided to raise horses was to get together a herd of Thoroughbred horses like they had raised on the plantation where he had grown up. Shortly after his arrival to Texas, he learned that they weren't really suitable as cow ponies. And most of the horses you'd sell in Texas would be cow ponies these days. So he got the idea that he could get a Thoroughbred stallion and a herd of mustang mares and see what kind of colt he'd get. But after seeing the buckskin stallion, he knew he couldn't find anything to use for a stud that could compare with him.

It dawned on him that he hadn't named him. The name you think of for a buckskin horse was Buck. But the buckskin gelding he had bought a year before was already named Buck. The buckskin stallion had a very masculine build, but he also had a lot of scars from battles with other stallions. So Jim decided a fitting name for him would be Hercules. That was what he called him.

While Jim was riding around the horse herd, he was looking over the mares. You normally didn't bother to break mares to ride in cow country. A cowboy would get laughed off the range if he was seen riding a mare. They were used for breeding stock only. But there was an exception to this. If a bronc buster saddle broke a mare and gentled her down for a woman to ride, then it was socially acceptable. And Jim knew that Vickie preferred to ride a mare. So he was looking for a mare that he thought might be a good choice for Vickie.

At the other end of the horse herd, Jim saw He Who Flies. He was out looking at the horses too. He Who Flies would ride out and look the horses over periodically. Jim halted his horse alongside of He Who Flies and told him what he had named the herd stallion. Then he explained he was looking for a mare to gentle down for his bride to be.

He Who Flies explained that if you cut a mare out of the herd, the stallion would get upset. The stallion considered himself to be their protector. So Jim asked him what he recommended. He Who Flies said if they herded the entire herd into the corral and if Jim saddled Hercules and mounted him, he would then stand still for He Who Flies to rope a mare and gentle her down so Jim could saddle her and start riding her.

So they ran the horses into the corral, and Jim picked out a beautiful red mare. He roped Hercules and tried to put a bridle on him, but he started fighting him. He jumped out of his way, pulled the rope across his front legs in the fashion he had seen He Who Flies do, and threw him. Then before he could get up, he breathed into his nostrils. Hercules calmed down almost immediately. Jim let him up and put a bridle on him and saddled him up. He mounted him and rode him around the corral a little bit. He had breathed in his nostrils shortly after He Who Flies had caught him, but it had been a while since he'd had any handling.

Then He Who Flies roped the red mare and started gentling her down. Jim unsaddled the stallion and turned him out with the rest of the horses but kept the mare in the corral. He started saddling her and riding her every day to get her used to being ridden and gentled down so that Vickie would have a horse to ride when she arrived at the ranch.

*****

He Who Flies got his little horse herd moving and headed west toward Indian country. He had notified Jim he wanted to return to his own people. Jim had paid him what he owed him with horses. He Who Flies avoided all the farms and ranches along the way. Jim had two cowboys go along with him just in case they did meet up with anyone. He Who Flies had a bill of sale for the horses in one of his saddlebags. Gil and Slim were the two cowboys sent to ride along with him to verify that He Who Flies was not a horse thief in case they encountered anyone along the route.

They went into the brush country. It was easier to stay hidden there. When they were beyond the frontier, the two cowboys bid him farewell and turned back to return to the ranch. He Who Flies headed north toward his village. He was on the borderline of Apache country but didn't expect any trouble. It was October. The farther north he got, the less likely it would be that he would encounter any enemy tribe. He had to travel several hundred miles to reach his village. He was in the rolling prairies now. When he stopped to camp at night, he built a fire out of buffalo chips and had a meal of boiled jerky and biscuits. The cook had taught him how to make biscuits and had given him some flour and baking powder to bring along. He still rode with a blanket only, but he did have a girth fastened around the horse this time with a saddle boot to carry his rifle. And he also had two saddlebags fastened to the saddle girth. He'd be a big man in his tribe with this many horses and a rifle to boot.

*****

Jim had hired some builders to come out and build a ranch house. He knew Vickie would have to have a decent house. He decided on one with three rooms at least and a nice stove and furniture. He still had plenty of money left over to live for a year at least and build a new house too.

207

He decided to go and visit Jack. He hadn't seen him in several months. He rode up into his yard late in the evening and said, "Hello, the house." And he noticed a bigger house than the one-room cabin he had seen the last time he was here.

To his surprise, Jeannie opened the door. He got down and tied his horse to the hitch rail and walked in.

Jack was sitting in an easy chair in the living room smoking a cigarette. He found that Jeannie was cooking supper.

"I think you've met my wife," Jack said.

"Well, yes, I have but didn't know you were married."

"Yep, we got married while you were off on your drive to Abilene that last time. I'd have invited you to the wedding if you had been here. You'll stay for supper, won't you?"

"Sure." Jim took off his hat and sat down in a chair near Jack.

"I'm getting married in about a month," Jim then said. "And you and Jeannie are invited to our wedding."

"Why, congratulations!" Jack replied.

"Who's the lucky girl?" Jeannie asked. She had come to the door to the living room with a stirring spoon in her hand.

"Vickie Allen. Do you know her?"

"Why, yes. I used to go buy supplies for the restaurant at the Allen store!"

They kept jawing while Jeannie finished cooking supper.

"Had any problem with rustlers?" Jim then asked.

"Nope, there wasn't any indication of rustlers this summer, but I had a few cowboys riding the range regularly to make sure there wasn't. We kept a branding crew going all summer, but I also hired some extra cowboys to patrol the range."

Then Jim explained about his problem with sleepers and his fight with rustlers. "I guess they didn't get as far as my ranch," Jack said. "So I've been lucky thus far."

After supper, Jim mounted his horse and rode back to his ranch. He put his horse in the corral and went to his cabin to go to bed. The ranch house was maybe half finished by now. He figured it should be done in time for his wedding in another month or so.

CHAPTER 43

Wedding

Jim and Ben had to push their horses to arrive in Waco on the fourteenth of November. Jim was leading the red mare. He had asked Ben to be his best man. So he had left Waylon in command at the ranch. Ben had announced his engagement to Jill. They were to get married the following June. But in the meantime, Jim was trying not to be late for his own wedding.

Vickie and her mother had finished making her wedding dress a week before. They had scheduled the wedding for the fifteenth as previously agreed. But here it was, the fourteenth, and no Jim. So Vickie went to the window to her bedroom that faced to the south. Their house was on the outskirts of town, so she could see the open range that extended to the horizon. Jim should come riding over that horizon.

She went back to the kitchen to help her mother cook supper. When she had to wait a minute or two to stir something, she went back to her bedroom and looked across toward the horizon again. Still no Jim.

Did he get killed by Indians? Or maybe some horse thief had shot him and stole his horse and just left him lying somewhere to die? She wondered if she could get her father to organize a search party to go and look for him.

Jim and Ben arrived in Waco after dark and checked into the hotel. Jim was aware of the superstition that a bridegroom wasn't supposed to see the bride on the day before the wedding.

The next morning, Jim and Ben went and had breakfast at the hotel restaurant. They waited until time for the stores to open and then went over to Mr. Allen's store. Mr. Allen sold both groceries and dry goods in his store. Jim and Ben decided they'd see if he had a broadcloth suit that would fit them.

When they walked into the store, Vickie wasn't there, but they saw Mr. Allen right away. Mr. Allen looked at him and breathed an audible sigh of relief. Jim walked over to him and shook hands with him. He introduced him to Ben and then told him what they needed. Mr. Allen quickly started looking at the ready-to-wear suits he had in stock. He didn't have one to fit Jim, but he told Jim which store to go to where he could find one. He had one that fit Ben okay. And Jim bought a sidesaddle for the red mare.

The wedding was scheduled for 2:00 p.m. that afternoon. It was Saturday, and Mr. Allen closed his store at noon. Vickie was flooded with relief when she found out that Jim did make it to town, but she wondered why he didn't tell her the night before to save her some worry.

At 2:25 p.m., Jim, Ben, Jill (Vickie's maid of honor), and Vickie were standing side by side at the front of the church with the minister performing their marriage ceremony. The glow on Vickie's face made it clear that any worries she had the previous day were totally forgotten.

After the service, Vickie went to a back room of the church and changed from her wedding dress to one more suitable for traveling.

When they left the church, Jim led Vickie to the red mare. He didn't have a carriage, but he helped her up into the saddle.

"Why, she's beautiful!" Vickie exclaimed. "What's her name?"

"I have haven't named her yet. I wanted you to name her."

"Her name will be Red. She's such a beautiful shade of red," Vickie decided.

They didn't ride off into the sunset because Killeen was almost due south of Waco, and that's where Jim intended to spend the night. The sun was getting lower over to their right. Scamp was riding in one of Vickie's saddlebags with his little head sticking out. Jim had put him in the left saddlebag. Vickie was riding on his right. Jim had made arrangements for one of the men to take a wagon back to the Allen house and load up her personal belongings and take them to the ranch. They'd probably arrive there by the time he and Vicki did.

ABOUT THE AUTHOR

Randell K. Whaley grew up in the Great Plains area, was a Navy pilot in Vietnam, has visited ten foreign countries, and has traveled extensively throughout most of the United States.

He has also been a cattle rancher and a teacher of programming in college for twelve years.

He currently lives in Dimmit, Texas.